KING ARTHUR
AND HIS KNIGHTS

Illustrated by Harry Theaker

TIGER BOOKS INTERNATIONAL
LONDON

KING
ARTHUR
AND HIS KNIGHTS

LIST OF ILLUSTRATIONS

CONTENTS

INTRODUCTION

The legends of King Arthur and his knights are among the best-loved of all the stories in the English language. This beautiful traditional story recounts the tales of Sir Lancelot and Sir Galahad, the flower of chivalry, as they rescue damsels in distress, defend the castles of their king and friend, and encounter fairies, witches, and enchanted animals in the magical forests and lakes.

Merlin the wizard, son of a beautiful Princess and a handsome fairy-man, works his wondrous magic on all around him and advises the young King in the wise ways that make his court at Camelot the most famous in the land. The story of the famous Round Table around which the knights meet is spellbinding, as are the exciting, sometimes wondrous, often daunting, adventures of the other, less well-known knights, such as the handsome Pig-Sty Prince who risked his life bravely in order to win the hand of the Princess he loved from her cruel and unreasonable father. Sir Gawaine wins the right to guard the enchanted Fairy Fountain, and the beautiful and blameless young Sir Perceval, the youngest son of

King Pellinore, friend of King Arthur, is appointed to sit next to the empty Seat Perilous to await the coming of Sir Galahad.

The evil deeds of Arthur's sister, the half-fairy Morgan-la-Fée, and the defeat of her Black Knight by the King, work their magic on young and old alike.

Many of the characters in the stories are related to one another and all their lives are intertwined. The chart below will help to explain the kinships of some of the more important characters.

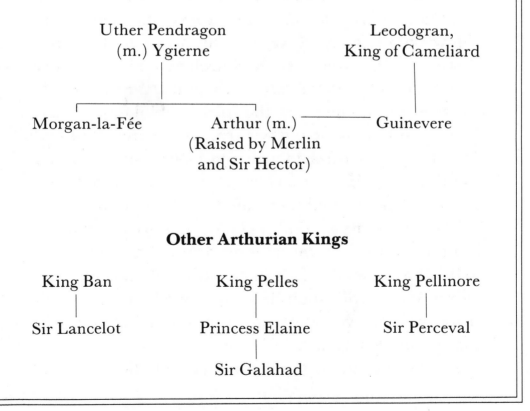

Uther Pendragon
(m.) Ygierne

Leodogran,
King of Cameliard

Morgan-la-Fée   Arthur (m.)   Guinevere
(Raised by Merlin
and Sir Hector)

Other Arthurian Kings

King Ban   King Pelles   King Pellinore

Sir Lancelot   Princess Elaine   Sir Perceval

Sir Galahad

CHAPTER ONE
MERLIN

t was midnight. On top of a high mountain, hundreds of wicked fairy-men were sitting or standing in strange shadowy groups under the tiny light of a new moon. They were talking eagerly and gloomily among themselves. Below them were the dim houses of the villages, with many a shadowy church tower rising above the roofs. And the wicked fairy-men were saying to each other that there were too many such churches, and that every good man or good woman in the human world made the power of themselves, the spirits of evil, grow less.

A terrible-looking old wizard, with a face dark and knotted, and with a long white beard, spoke louder than the rest. He was as clever as he was wicked, and all the others hushed their talk to listen to him.

"What we must do," said he, "is to persuade a human maiden to marry one of us. Their children will, of course, be half men and half fairies. The eldest child will soon belong entirely to us, and, through him, we can regain the power in the world that we are losing so fast."

All the wicked fairy-men nodded their heads.

"Good! Good!" they said, all together, "Very good!"

The terrible old wizard glanced around the circle of dim moonlit faces in search of one that was nice-looking. But each was uglier than the last.

"A lovely Princess lives in the castle on the opposite side of the valley," he declared. "But I do not think she would be likely to fall in love with one of *us*!"

Then a dark fairy-man stepped out from the rest. He was one of the youngest among them. He had just celebrated his thousandth birthday. His long, lean hands were like bird's claws as he held them up to command attention.

"I know something of the Princess," said he. "She is careless. And now and then she goes to sleep without asking our greatest enemies, the white spirits of the air, to protect her."

"Ah-h-h-h!" hissed all the wicked fairy-men together. "Then she puts herself in our power!"

The awful old wizard chuckled with delight. "Go quickly!" he cried. "Put on your bat's wings and fly to her window! If the white spirits of the air are not there, you will be able to get in and change yourself into anything you like!"

So the bad fairy-man fastened on his bat's wings and swept over the valley. A jewelled lamp was set in the Princess's window, but there were no white spirits hovering near. The little Princess had gone to bed, forgetting all about them.

So the fairy-man slipped in at the open casement. And there, the sweetest maiden in the world lay fast asleep.

He tiptoed up to her, a dark, mysterious, cruel shadow. Then, all at once, she opened her eyes and saw him. But the good spirits were very far away and could not show him as he really was. And the Princess smiled and lay looking at him. She was half-dreaming; and, in her dream, the old bad fairy-man seemed to be a beautiful gold-clad Prince. He lifted her in his arms and carried her to the window-sill. And then all the other wicked fairy-men came flapping through the castle on their great dark wings. But the little Princess was still dreaming of the beautiful Fairy Prince and of a wonderful palace, built of gold and mother-o'-pearl, where he lived with magnificently dressed courtiers to wait on him. In this dream she married him with all the proper fairy ceremonies and sat with him on his throne.

Night after night, the Princess dreamed this, but always forgot all about her dream in the daytime. At last, she seemed to go to sleep for a much longer time than usual, and to dream that a wonderful fairy-child was born.

Then, in her dream, there came to her for the first time the memory of the white spirits of the air. And she told the Fairy Prince, and all his courtiers, that the little baby must be christened.

Behold! A great clap of thunder shook the air! The golden light changed to darkness and the Prince and his courtiers into strange and terrible beings with wide black wings like bats. They flew hither and thither in a whirring, angry crowd. The Princess woke in terror, to find herself alone, shut up in a deserted tower, with nobody near but the fairy baby upon her knees.

She began to cry bitterly, when lo! a little, soft, kind voice came from the rosy mouth of the tiny thing on her lap.

"Don't cry," said the baby. "I know a way to help you. And through me, all sorts of wonderful things will come to pass."

Then a step came up the long winding stair, the door opened, and a good and holy man called Blaise, who looked at her gravely, but very kindly, stood on the threshold.

"Oh, Blaise! Dear Blaise!" cried the poor little Princess. "What has happened?"

"My little Princess," said Blaise, "it is for *you* to tell us. Strange stories are being told about you. People say that *you* have been, for many months, in the power of the wicked fairy-men who live on the mountain. And they declare that you have been married to one of them, secretly, and that the little baby in your arms is the son, not of a baptized human Prince, but of a Prince of wickedness and darkness."

Then the Princess cried more bitterly than ever and told Blaise all about it.

Blaise hurried off, and came back with a silver chalice full of water drawn from a well where the white spirits might often be seen flying about at sunset. And, then and there, he christened the little fairy baby – naming him Merlin. And when the water from the well sparkled in bright drops all among the baby's golden hair, little Merlin laughed and shouted with gladness.

"I am a human baby now!" he cried. "But still I know things that other human babies will never know! And, when I grow up, I shall be able to use all sorts of wonderful powers that I have inherited from the fairy-men of the high mountain. But I shall use them for good, and not for evil. For, through me, a Round Table shall be given to a great King, and many knights shall sit around it, and the deeds these knights shall do will be blessed by the poor and the weak and helpless, and sung by golden-mouthed poets for hundreds and hundreds of years!"

Then Blaise led the little Princess back to her own chamber, where the white spirits who loved her flew, like snowy birds, backwards and forwards before the window, so that the wicked fairy-men of the mountain were never again able to get in.

CHAPTER TWO

THE WHITE DRAGON
AND THE RED

Merlin, the wonderful baby, grew up into a handsome youth, but nobody quite understood him, and a good many people were rather afraid of him. He never did naughty or cruel things, but he would often rock his sides with laughter for what seemed to be no reason at all. Sometimes he would disappear for a week or two, and it was whispered of him that he used to catch and ride the wild stags, and that, when he rode a great antlered beauty, all the pretty does and their young followed him, so that the forest-glades seemed alive with flying herds of deer. The gossips said, too, that the fairy people were building a house for Merlin in the deep green places of the woods – a house with seventy windows and sixty doors, where as soon as he was old enough he would live, quite alone. But when Merlin was stared at, on account of these things, he only laughed to himself, as usual, and went about his business unconcernedly.

Then, one day, a party of horsemen came riding along towards the palace in which Merlin had been born. They kept asking where they could find a cer-

Chapter Two: The White Dragon and the Red

The boy Merlin was led before the King,
the cruel and selfish Vortigern. After
Merlin showed the wicked ruler the
enchanted lake beneath the earth,
Vortigern understood why his workmen
had been unable to build a tower as he
wished.

Chapter Two: The White Dragon and the Red

The fight between the dragons, witnessed only by Vortigern, was in fact a battle between the white dragon representing the soul of the king's strongest enemy and the red dragon, the shadow of Vortigern himself.

tain handsome youth of whom all sorts of strange
things were said. And, sure enough, as they drew rein
before the gate of the city, there stood the slender
boy, with his laughing mouth, and eyes so clear and
free.

One of the horsemen sprang down, seized Merlin,
and flung him on to his own saddle. Then he sprang
up behind, set spurs to his steed, and galloped off in
company with his friends. Merlin neither struggled
nor cried out. He just laughed to himself; for, ever
since he was a baby, he had known that this would
happen to him.

On went the party of horsemen at full speed, until
they came to a country far from Merlin's home. Between the mountain passes they rode, and presently
they came out upon a low plain, where a lot of workmen were toiling, and toiling, to build a great tower.
They had brought hundreds of stones together,
which were lying about broken, or piled into mud-
dled heaps. Men on horseback rode to and fro, calling out directions, or rebuking the workmen for their
carelessness. The poor workmen staggered about,
placing the stones one on the top of the other. But,
however careful they were, the stones all fell down
again!

Watching the work from a grassy mound stood a
tall man dressed for battle, with a crown on his head,
and a cruel, yet a frightened face below the crown.

Behind him waited a standard-bearer, dressed in royal purple. Over his crowned head floated the flag that had floated over many a prince of a long, long line of kings.

The company of horsemen galloped up to the mound. Taking Merlin down from the horse, they led him, bound, up to the cruel-eyed monarch who stood there.

"Is this the boy?" asked the King.

"Yes, sire," answered the rider who had first seized Merlin.

The King looked steadily and fiercely at Merlin, who smiled quite pleasantly, not at all afraid.

"You laugh, child!" said the King, with a heavy frown. "You do not know your fate! Do you see those stones where men have built the foundations of a great tower?"

Merlin nodded. He looked around at the heaps of unused stones, so many of which were broken and ruined.

"In that tower," went on the King, "I mean to find a safe refuge from the terrible enemies who swarm around my country and who will, assuredly, ride over the mountains one day. Unless I take the necessary precautions, they will conquer my kingdom and kill me. Only a strong tower can be my haven. But, though I have tried for many months to build it, no sooner are the stones set up than they all fall down again!"

"Very likely! Very likely!" said Merlin.

"Wait!" growled the King like angry thunder. "I was told by a magician that only the blood of a youth of whom it was said he was half a fairy could give firmness to the foundations of the tower. You, I understand, are that unhappy child! My tower I must have, though your blood has to be spilled in order to build it!"

Even this cruel King looked unhappy as well as frightened as he spoke. But, for all his sorrow and his fear, he was quite determined to kill Merlin, so that he could go on building his tower.

Merlin laughed, bowed, and sat himself down on the grass of the mound.

"So? So?" said he. "But even my blood, great King, will not help you to build a tower on the top of a lake of water!"

The King frowned with perplexity, and stared.

"Lake of water! What do you mean?" he demanded. "There is no lake here."

"Have your workmen dig around the foundations of your unfinished, tumbling-down tower, and you will soon see for yourself," laughed Merlin, rocking himself to and fro.

The King – whose name was Vortigern – was so amazed that he actually did as the strange mocking boy told him! He sent for the architect and then ordered him to have the workmen dig around the foundations with their spades. So the workmen stopped trying to set up the stones and started digging out the soil instead. And, behold! almost immediately they were digging in mud. Then, up bubbled the hidden water through the mud, and down fell the banks of the ditches, followed by all the stones that had not tumbled down before. And, as the stones and banks slipped down, more and more water rushed up, till at last the whole of the middle of the plain was one great lake.

Then the King turned to Merlin, more afraid, now, of this strange boy than of all the people who, he expected, would come riding over the hills to kill him.

"What does it all mean?" he asked, trembling.

Merlin shook his head. Suddenly tears sprang to his eyes and rolled down his cheeks. He was sorry for the cruel King, even though Vortigern had never been sorry for *him*.

"There is a great stone below the lake," he said, in a whisper. "Two dragons sleep there – a red one and a white. One day, they will come out from under the stone and meet on the waters of the lake in a fearful battle. In the white dragon is the soul of your strongest enemy – in the red dragon, Vortigern, you may see the shadow of yourself."

Then Merlin stepped down from the mound and went slowly away, and nobody tried to hold him. But

Vortigern sat on the grass and stared for an entire week at the still green waters of the magical lake.

And at last, while he stared, he saw the waters shudder and shake into great waves. The waves sprang higher and higher, like horses tossing their white and shaggy manes. Then up through the hills and valleys of the storm-lashed water came the white dragon and the red. The white dragon was as pale as snow, and the red dragon was as scarlet as blood. And from end to end of the fairy lake, they fought each other, until, with a great cry the red dragon fell dead upon the beach, among the green rushes and the broken stems of the water-flowers.

Vortigern rose and fled. But he thought he heard the voice of the fairy-boy echoing all around about him as he went:

"In the white dragon is the soul of your strongest enemy – in the red dragon, Vortigern, you may see the shadow of yourself!"

The King reached his palace quaking with fear, but lo! his courtiers came running to tell him that the lake had sunk back deep into the earth, and that now the workmen were building his tower as fast as ever they could. So Vortigern began his old, cruel, wicked ways once more. Then, as soon as the tower was finished, he shut himself up in it for safety. But at night, very often, he woke up panting with terror, for, in his dreams he still saw the mighty battle between the white dragon and the red.

And, surely enough, one day his strongest enemy came over the hills with a great army, for Vortigern's people, racked with their King's wickedness and cruelty, had sent out a pitiful cry for help. The King who rode over the hills was great and good, and he rescued the unhappy people and killed Vortigern. So this King reigned over the kingdom in his place. His name was Uther Pendragon. The reasons for this name and some of the things that he did you will read about in another story.

CHAPTER THREE
THE SHINING CUP

ong before Merlin was born there lived, in an Eastern country, a good and holy man called Joseph, who had, for many years, been the guardian of a wonderful Cup. Nobody quite knew where his Cup had first come from, nor what it was that gave it the lovely radiance which always surrounded it. But all Joseph's friends knew that the Cup was a great treasure, and that only a good and faithful man could have been chosen as its guardian.

This Cup was called the Grail Cup, and sometimes Joseph would summon his children and his grand-children (for he was quite an old man), and the best-loved of his friends, to take their seats at a silver table, which he had himself made, in the middle of which he would set the Grail Cup. Then, while everyone looked at the shining mist in which the Cup was half hidden, Joseph would tell another good man whom he loved very dearly, called Alan, to go to a certain stream and catch a silver fish that he would see swimming about in the clear water. Alan would go willingly; and, however often he went, he always saw the silver fish gleaming and flashing among the singing bubbles of the stream. He would catch the fish and bring it to the bright table to show to Joseph, who would then tell him to take it and cook it on a fire of clear embers. When this was done, Alan served the fish to the people who sat about the silver table. No matter how many there were to feed, the fish always went around, and, when the feast was over, everybody who had shared in it felt happy, content, and joyful, strong to do what was right and to resist what was wrong. They would go away glad and grateful, wondering how it was that Alan could always catch so magical and wonderful a fish, and they gave him the name of the Rich Fisher. But wicked men ruled the country in which Joseph lived. They were plotting against him, when, one day, as he worked in his garden, he was visited by a beautiful spirit, who told him that he must take the Grail to a distant country, called West-over-the-Sea. Joseph asked how this could be done, "For," said he, "I have no ship in which to travel." The bright spirit, however, told him to have faith. He should just set off with his children and his friends, and they were to carry the silver table and the Shining Cup with them. Then the vision faded and Joseph, sending for the Rich Fisher, told him, and everybody else, to make ready for the journey.

Well, they set off as soon as they could. They carried the silver table carefully, and Joseph bore the

Shining Cup. After journeying for many days, they reached the seashore. Joseph stood at the edge of the water, perplexed and wondering; and then a voice suddenly floated across the shore.

"Take off your white under-robe, Joseph, and spread it upon the sea."

Joseph heard the voice, and, while his people gazed in wonder, he took off his white under-robe and spread the soft hand-sewn linen out upon the water. It floated like a beautiful raft. Then, Joseph heard the voice a second time.

"Stand upon it, and let your people follow you."

Joseph moved forward. Lifting the casket which held the Grail Cup up high, he stepped upon this strange white boat. The linen garment was firm to his feet. It rocked up and down like a strong ship at anchor. He stood there, fearless and upright, and called to all his people to join him. In twos and threes they came, amazed but trustful, bringing with them the silver table. They found that there was room for everyone, and in a few minutes, the strange boat was sailing smoothly across the ocean.

The sun sank, the moon rose, and still the white linen robe sailed, faster than any ship, over the starlit water. Then, by and by, the moon set, too, and the sun came up again into the sky behind the voyagers. As it rose, Joseph cried out, joyfully, that he could see the sandy beaches, the high cliffs, and the distant mountains of West-over-the Sea.

Surely enough, there lay the land, sparkling and beautiful. But, as they drew nearer, they saw that while they had left warmth, and flowers, and fruiting trees behind them, they had come to a country where winter reigned. All was cold and snow-covered. The outspread robe floated into a little bay, and one by one, the voyagers hurried to the shore.

Joseph came last of all, and, as he left his strange ship, the voice came again, down from the mountains, telling him to lift his robe and put it once more upon his shoulders. He did so, and, behold! it was quite warm and dry. Then he and the Rich Fisher led all the people up a narrow pathway which climbed the cliffside. And still Joseph carried the Grail, while some of the others willingly carried the silver table.

They reached the top of the cliff, and then they set off again, over mountains and through valleys, until they reached a place called Glastonbury. And Joseph knew that here he was meant to build a little church of wood. He leaned on his staff for a long time, looking around. It seemed to him a wonderful thing that he was to build a church in the island of Britain, which was the real name of West-over-the-Sea.

Then, as he leaned on his staff, he felt it move and tremble strangely under his hand. He glanced down, and lo! he saw little twigs and stems sprouting out on all sides of it, laden with green leaves and pale whitethorn flowers. It had rooted in the frost-bound earth! Then the staff shot upward, and great boughs, all covered with blossom, branched above his head. In a few minutes, he was standing, amazed, under a spreading thorn tree, laden with sweet-smelling, snow-white bloom!

Then Joseph told them to set down the silver table under the flowering tree. They did so, and the Rich Fisher went to a half-frozen stream close by and caught a little silver fish quickly, and, making a fire of sticks, roasted it upon the clear embers. There, under the blossoming thorn tree, the children and followers of Joseph and the Rich Fisher ate their first banquet at West-over-the-Sea, while the snow fell thickly.

Now, while they were feasting, an old man dressed in a long robe, who was called a Druid, passed by, and paused, amazed at what he saw. While he watched, the banquet came to an end. The strangers stood up, and, unaware that they were seen by the old Druid, they all swept away, in a radiant procession, towards the inland forests, leaving the blossoming tree standing, mysterious and beautiful, under the falling snow.

Then the Druid went back to the grove of oaks in which he lived and wrote down all that he had seen in a parchment book with gold clasps to it. This book he locked up, and it was kept hidden for many years; but

Merlin heard of it. One day, long, long afterwards, he came to Glastonbury, found it, and read it. What he did, after he had read the book, you will be told in another story.

But meanwhile Joseph, and the Rich Fisher, and their friends, sought the King of the country, and he gave them the piece of land where the thorn tree was blossoming, for their own. So they built a little wooden church.

CHAPTER FOUR
KING MORDRAIN'S PERILOUS ISLAND

t the time the Grail Cup was carried to Britain, many strange things took place all over the world. One of the strangest was an adventure which happened to a heathen King called Mordrain, who had known Joseph, and had become a Christian on account of the things that Joseph had taught him. One day when Mordrain was out hunting, his horses took fright at the thunder and lightning of a great storm. They galloped off with the chariot in which the King sat; he would have been killed had not a mysterious hand and arm, like the hand and arm of a giant, come out of one of the blackest clouds, lifted him bodily, swing him through the storm-filled air, and set him down on an island in the middle of the ocean!

The island was nothing but a great pile of rugged rocks, with caves running deep within them. King Mordrain was terribly hungry; and, as he climbed over the rocks, he thought he would certainly die of famine and thirst. Suddenly he caught sight of the prettiest little ship in the world, fluttering like a butterfly out of the blackness of the storm. Mast, sails, and rigging were all lily-white, and a red cross, like the cross that you may see nowadays on the banner of St. George of England, floated just above the bow. Under the crimson cross, a man with a kind, beautiful face stood erect, gazing towards the desolate island.

This pretty red-and-white ship came sailing on and paused at last almost at the feet of the astonished King. As it lay, moving softly up and down, the man struck a harp which he held, and began to sing. While he sang, it seemed as if a delicious fragrance floated from the ship, so that Mordrain felt as if he stood in a valley of wild flowers. He shut his eyes, and he thought that sweet cool grass was springing up about his feet and that trees with rosy apples on them grew within reach of his hand; and that, farther still, sleek gentle cows were walking homeward to be milked. Still the man in the bow of the ship sang on; and then Mordrain thought that he was drinking the cows' sweet milk, biting joyfully into the red apples, and eating white delicate bread. All the time, the song continued, and the King caught the echo of the words.

"I am the minstrel who sails the seas from port to port. I make beautiful the things which once were ugly and vile. I give riches to the poor, health to the sick, happiness to the sorrowful! To you, O sad and weary King, I give refreshing food and drink of which

Chapter Three: The Shining Cup

An old man dressed in a long robe passed by and stopped, utterly amazed by what he saw. A group of people from the East, in blue and purple and scarlet robes, were seated around a shining silver table under the shade of a tree all covered with flowers.

Chapter Four: King Mordrain's Perilous Island

Under the red cross, a man stood gazing toward the perilous rocks. His kind face and his beautiful singing astonished King Mordrain, stranded alone on the mysterious island.

you are in need!"

The song ceased, and Mordrain opened his eyes. Nothing could be seen but the salt ocean, the cruel rocks, and the little white ship with the man who sang in the bow. But Mordrain felt as if he had just risen from the most delicious feast in the world! His eyes were bright, and he stood upright, strong and happy. But, just as he was going to beg the minstrel to land, the whole ship vanished from sight! Instead of the delicate white sails and the glowing red cross, Mordrain now saw another ship driving fast through the water, out of the north. This vessel was richly fitted and inlaid with thousands of jewels. Its sails were like black velvet; and, under their mysterious shadow, sat the most beautiful woman the King had ever seen.

This woman, too, was singing as the ship drove in among the rocks. But Mordrain, listening, knew that her song was evil. She sang of a palace where she reigned as Queen, to which she wanted to carry the King in her boat. She promised him wealth, and ease, and luxury. All the time she sang, the lightning flashed upon the jewels on the mast and rigging; the thunder pealed and rolled and muttered. Over and over again, Mordrain was on the point of stepping on to the boat and telling the beautiful wicked woman that he would sail away with her to her own land. But something always held him back.

At last, as a vivid lightning flash wrapped all the ship in blue flame while the thunder crashed like cannon, the song suddenly ceased. When Mordrain's eyes were cleared from the blindness which had fallen upon them for a moment's space, both ship and singer had vanished.

Great waves were breaking over the rocks now, and the King took shelter in a deep cave. All night, he heard the seas and winds roaring, but, towards morning, both sky and water became calm. Mordrain fell asleep, and dreamed that, once more, he stood in the valley of flowers. Waking up, he smelled their fragrance. Peeping out of his cave, he saw, again, the pretty ship rocking in the cove, with its lily-white sails, its red cross, and its minstrel making music on his harp.

Mordrain hurried down the rocks to meet him and told him of the beautiful evil woman on the ship with the black sails. The minstrel listened gravely; when the King had finished his story, he told him that the woman was really a demon in disguise, who would have flung him into the sea and left him to perish.

"And, King Mordrain," said the minstrel, "you are one of those who have been chosen to follow the Grail-People into West-over-the-Sea, and to find the hiding-place in which the Shining Cup has been safely placed by Joseph. But you must never follow any leader, nor sail from this island in any ship, unless you see the cross that one day will shine red upon the white banner of England. That banner, only, is the true banner for you – that sign, only, the true sign which will lead you to the hiding place of the Cup that people know as the *Holy* Grail."

The minstrel and the ship vanished once more, but Mordrain was left refreshed and comforted.

Another day passed, night came, and the King slept calmly in his cave. He went out just as the morning star was fading, and, behold! a third ship was sailing towards the island.

Mordrain gazed, and gazed, and suddenly his face grew radiant with delight. He recognized the ship – it had lain always at anchor in his own royal bay! Familiar forms of his own courtiers crowded in the bows – familiar faces were turned upon him, familiar voices called and shouted his name! King Mordrain waved his hands and shouted back to the courtiers. Only for one moment did he pause before leaping down the rocks to meet his friends – only for one moment, to look, and look in vain, for the banner with the red cross upon it.

"It is not there! But what can it matter? This is my own royal vessel; these are my own courtiers and servants!"

The King thrust away the thought of the red cross, and, still calling his glad greetings, sprang on to the deck of the ship. Suddenly he paused – a feeling of terror seized him the moment that his foot touched the boards. Suddenly, a clap of thunder sounded, and everybody on the ship vanished. King Mordrain was left on the ship, without pilot, sailors, sails, or rigging.

King Mordrain called aloud upon the beautiful minstrel to save him. Then, out of the blue distance, came two birds like shining eagles, and they carried a knight, with a wonderful, compassionate face, between them. They paused near Mordrain's terrible ship, and the knight with the brave gentle face stooped towards the water and seemed to trace something upon the waves. Mordrain thought that, under the white foam of the sea, he saw the red cross that, he had been told, would shine one day on the white banner of St. George.

Then the knight called to the King. He told him to take the rudder and follow the flight of the birds, for he was Mordrain's appointed guardian and would lead him to safety. And the two great birds turned westward, and Mordrain followed them, carried mysteriously in the ship without sailors and without sails, until he reached West-over-the-Sea. There he landed on the shore on the very spot where Joseph and the Rich Fisher had landed with the silver table and the Shining Cup of the Holy Grail.

CHAPTER FIVE

THE FIERY STAR

ne dark and stormy night, Merlin stood at one of his windows, and kept looking up at the wild sky. He was expecting to see something there: something very unusual and wonderful, which one of his fairy books had told him to expect. For a long time, however, nothing happened. Then, all at once, he caught sight of a little pearly glimmer in the north. This little pearly glimmer grew brighter and brighter; it turned from silver to gold, and from gold to a deep shining red. Merlin gazed still more eagerly, and presently, in the heart of the red glow, he saw a great star brighten, as you might see a crimson fire suddenly break into a shining flame. From the great star, one ray shot out suddenly, brilliant as a diamond and slender as a knight's spear. At the end of the ray appeared a globe of fire, which, as Merlin still watched, uncoiled itself slowly and took the shape of a beautiful and terrible dragon. This fiery dragon opened its mouth and sent out two more rays, one to the east, the other to the west. The eastern ray seemed to have no end to it, but disappeared in brightness, so that you might almost have thought the sun was just going to rise. The ray to the west went into the night shadows and then broke up into seven smaller rays, which spread themselves in a golden fan above the shadowy peaks of the distant hills.

When Merlin had seen all this happen, he laughed gladly, and flying down the long staircase of his fairy home as lightly as a bird or a butterfly, he set off on invisible wings through the night. Always the fiery dragon shone in the sky overhead; and Merlin knew that its bright form was hanging just over the castle of Uther, the King. As the wizard drew near to the castle, he dropped to his feet on the grass and took on the form of an old man, wrapped in a cloak. With his white beard, he walked up to the castle gates and knocked loudly with his staff.

Now, all this time, the great flaming dragon was lying, stretched out in the sky, steeping the towers and turrets of the castle in a crimson light, fiery and terrible. The guards and servants, the porters, the cooks, and the pages had seen it and were frightened out of their wits. Nobody dared to answer the door at first, so Merlin knocked again, much more loudly. Then, when a terrified porter appeared, the magician, in a voice of authority, demanded to be taken to the presence of the King.

There was something in Merlin's voice that the porter dared not disobey. He hurriedly opened the great gate and let the old man in. Then he led Merlin through the courtyard – all lit up by the dragon – down the great stone corridor, across the hall, hung with gorgeous tapestry, where terrified pages waited, dressed in satins and silks. Then the porter paused and pointed. Merlin went on alone, right into the royal apartment of the King.

King Uther sat on his throne, pale and grave, and quite alone. Through a great window, curtainless and arched, came the fiery glow from the dragon in the sky. It stained the fresh green rushes on the floor with crimson and shone all around the solitary figure of the King. Uther looked up at the sound of footsteps and saw an old man coming slowly up the room, wrapped in a long cloak, with a snow-white beard.

"Who are you? Why do you come here unbidden and unannounced?" demanded the King sternly. But, before he finished speaking, the old man threw back his cloak, and Uther saw who he was.

"Merlin – my friend Merlin!" he cried in an altered voice. "I am indeed glad you have come! What means this blazing and terrible dragon in the sky?"

Then Merlin answered. His voice sounded so glad and triumphant that King Uther knew the news was good even before the magician gave it.

"The dragon is the most wonderful sign that has ever shone in the sky above the castle of a King," cried Merlin. "I have been watching for it night after night! It means that to you, and to the beautiful lady you love, a little Prince will be born. This little Prince will be the greatest King the world ever saw. He will reign over many subjects and will conquer all his enemies. He is the ray from the mouth of the dragon that goes to the east, and he will be as bright and beautiful as the rising sun. The ray that goes to the west, and breaks up into seven rays, is your daughter. She will be, not only a Princess, but a fairy, and have seven fairy children, who will teach the men-children of the West the songs that fairies sing. That is the meaning of the fiery dragon, King Uther – the meaning that I have hurried into your presence to explain!"

Uther listened breathlessly, and, all the time, the light from the dragon shone crimson upon the faces, and hands, and robes, of the old wizard and the young King. Then Uther leaned forward and pressed his fingers on Merlin's arm.

"My beautiful lady?" he said eagerly. "Do you mean Ygierne?"

He could hardly wait for Merlin's reply, because he had loved Ygierne for months, but she was shut up in a castle, quite out of his reach.

"Yes, I mean Ygierne," answered Merlin. "I promise that you shall have her for your bride. I promise, too, that you and she shall have this bright and beautiful Prince and this fairy-like Princess for your children. But, if you are to marry Ygierne through my help, you must make me a promise in return."

"What is that?" asked Uther. "Tell me! There is no promise that I would not make for the sake of beautiful Ygierne!"

"You must promise that, as soon as your little son is born, you will give him into my care. He has a great work to do in the world and can only learn to do it if I have the charge of him. Give me *your* promise, Uther, and I will set about the performance of *mine*!"

Then King Uther, for a moment, felt uncertain and sad. Where would be the gladness in a little princely son, if the child was to be taken away from him as soon as he was born? But he loved Ygierne so passionately that, after only hesitating for one second, he consented.

"Very well, Merlin!" he cried. "Very well! You shall have my little son to bring up as your own child, if you will only make it possible for me to marry my beautiful lady, Ygierne!"

The red glow shining through the window, which fell from the fiery dragon in the sky, grew stronger and fiercer as Uther spoke. When he had given the promise, the light blazed crimson and terrible about the throne on which he sat and showed up all the diamonds and sapphires in his crown. A peal of thunder rolled above the palace; a flash of lightning darted about the great stone towers. The blazing dragon seemed to close its jaws. As it closed them, the rays drew slowly back into its great mouth. It stretched out its long, fiery claws, and two great golden wings rose, waving, over its great golden head. Then, all at once, it struck its wings together once – twice – thrice. Once, twice, thrice, the thunder pealed out again; before its echoes had died away, the fiery creature had shot, swift as an arrow, far through the night sky, leaving a long tail of starry light, like the tail of a comet, behind it.

Even King Uther had crouched for a moment and covered his face. When he took his jewelled satin cloak away from his eyes, the royal throne room was empty, dark, and still. Merlin had vanished with the dragon.

The King stepped down from his throne and went to the window. He looked up to the sky, and saw it dark and clear, silvered over with quiet little stars. Then he summoned a herald and told him to take his trumpet and go through the castle, crying aloud these words:

"King Uther has been told the meaning of the blazing dragon in the sky. It is a sign of great gladness, and victory, and well-being for himself and for his kingdom. From this moment, the King will be known as King Uther Pendragon, and he lays commands on his royal sculptors that two golden dragons immediately be made. One of these dragons will be set in the capital of his kingdom. The other will be carried by his royal standard-bearer into every battle. These are the orders of Uther Pendragon, King of the Lordly and ancient country of Britain!"

CHAPTER SIX

THE ROUND TABLE
OF OAK

Merlin, the great wizard, was the best friend of Uther, the good King. The stories told about the magician's fairy house in the woods were quite true, and Merlin spent most of his time in his wonderful home among the pine-trees. What a strange shadowy place it was, to be sure, with wild deer feeding in the glades that surrounded it. Human beings never ventured very far into this mysterious wood, but they whispered all sorts of tales about it. They named it the Enchanted Forest, or sometimes, the Valley of No Return. Hunters who followed the hares over the meadows, or chased the wild boars through the tangled thickets on the edge of the woodland, always stopped short, and turned their horses and their hounds around, when the looked into the dark shadows of these haunted trees. Sometimes, they caught glimpses of dim walls and towers, and heard sounds like fairies singing, or unseen horses trampling, or invisible hounds baying through the wood. Then the real horses and hounds would begin to tremble as the hunters hurried them away. But nobody could ever quite describe what he had seen and heard, though all were agreed that, if any rash person ventured up to the dim walls of Merlin's home, he was pretty certain never to come back.

In this hidden house, then, Merlin learned all sorts of things from the fairies, because he could see and hear and speak to the invisible people of the air. He learned so many of their secrets that at last he became a regular fairy-king among them.

One day, Merlin was standing under a great oak tree, just after the sun had set and the quiet shadows had begun to steal through his beautiful wood. Merlin felt that something rather wonderful was going to happen – something beautiful and strange. The evening grew darker, and, all at once, the oak boughs above his head began to rustle and whisper, as if a little wind were moving them up and down. At the same time, he heard soft knockings inside the tree trunk, and a murmur of many voices speaking together in what seemed to be an unknown foreign tongue.

Then, in the middle of the shadows, the branches and trunk of the oak began to give out a silver shining, like the shining of a full moon. Slowly and silently, a great clearness grew around about the tree. The boughs seemed to fade away, and a wonderful picture appeared, painted on the bright air – the picture of an old man, with a long white beard, standing before a silver table on which was a mysterious and beautiful Shining Cup. Round about the table, many people were seated, who wore bright oriental robes. They looked very calm and content. And, by the side of the old man with the white beard, stood a younger man, with a silver fish in his hands. He placed the fish on the table, and everyone stood up. Merlin thought he heard them singing as they did so. Then the whole vision faded; and Merlin found himself alone in the forest again, with the oak leaves whispering and rustling above his head.

But, while he stood wondering, behold! a little book suddenly fell down from the branches right to his feet. As it fell, he heard a voice speaking among the leaves.

"In the little book is written the story of the silver table and the Shining Cup that you have been allowed to see in a vision! I, who speak to you, am the old Druid who saw them brought to the land of West-over-the-Sea. I have been commanded to show you the vision and to give you the little book. Also, I have been commanded to tell you that, from the wood of the oak tree in whose boughs you have seen the vision, you are to carve another Round Table, like the Silver Table on which the Shining Cup stood. When you have carved this second Round Table, you are to take it to King Uther, and bid him keep it carefully in his palace until his death. For it will have a wonderful meaning and purpose for many years to come."

Chapter Six: The Round Table of Oak

Merlin picked up the ancient book and took it to his fairy house in the enchanted forest. There, he lit his lamp, and sitting down among his magic volumes, he read the book from cover to cover.

The voice died away, and Merlin picked up the book and took it home to his fairy house. There he lit his lamp, and, sitting down among his magic volumes and crystals and strange boxes and chests, he read the book from end to end. In it was the whole story of Joseph and his followers, and the church made of wood at Glastonbury, and the beautiful Christmas-flowering thorn. Not only was the whole tale written down in the book, but there were also careful directions about the making of the second Round Table.

Merlin locked the book up carefully in one of his jewel boxes, for he knew what a very, very precious possession it was.

Merlin set to work to make a big Round Table from the oak tree in the wood. Nobody knows exactly how he made it, but the fairy folk helped him. When he had finished, he was even a greater magician than he had been when he had begun – so great that, by using certain spells, he was able to lift the Round Table straight out of his house in the Enchanted Forest and set it down in the very middle of the royal castle that belonged to Uther, the King.

Well, Uther was greatly amazed when he saw this beautiful and big Round Table, brought to his castle nobody knew how. As he gazed at it, however, he became aware that Merlin was standing by him, smiling at his astonishment. The magician told him something, though not all, of the way in which the table had been made; and Uther looked at him admiringly.

"You seem to me to be able to do anything you wish to, Merlin!" he exclaimed. "I wish you would bring me the Giants' Dance from Ireland!"

"What is the Giants' Dance?" asked Merlin. He knew quite well, really, but he was pretending that he did not.

King Uther told him, then, that he had just come back from a war in Ireland, and that, among the hills, there was an extraordinary circle of great stones, which the people said were enchanted giants, and which they always called the Giants' Dance. He had wished very much to bring this circle home with him and had set a whole army to work, to try and lift the stones from their places and set them on the ships that were waiting to carry them away. But, though all the engineers of those days had worked their hardest and done their best, none of them could lift the great stones so much as an inch out of the ground. In despair, Uther had given up the idea of bringing the stones to his own kingdom and had left them standing, in their wide, still, lonely magnificence, in the distant Irish hills.

"Oh!" said Merlin. "It's just a great circle of stones you want moving, is it? Well, that's easily done!"

Off he set for Ireland, with his crystal balls, and his

KING ARTHUR AND HIS KNIGHTS

black wands, and his lists of spells that were written down in his fairy books. But he left the small old book of the Holy Grail at home. When he reached the hill where the Giants' Dance stood, he went up to the top quite alone. What he said and did there, nobody ever knew! But the peasants who lived in huts in the valley told a strange story of what some of them had seen that night – a story about great stones that travelled, all alone and upright, down the slopes of the mountain, while voices, which guided their movements, called down from the air and up from the ground! They told, too, of great ships with shadowy sails that were seen setting out to sea. And the movements of the ships were guided by voices calling among the waves. However this might have been, whether the peasants really saw these things, or only dreamed them, it is certain that, the next morning, the Giants' Dance had been carried away from Ireland and set up, not very far from Uther's castle, on Salisbury Plain!

And on Salisbury Plain it stands to this day, but we call it Stonehenge now and have almost forgotten that it was once called the Giants' Dance. While, as for the Round Table, you may see a Round Table for yourselves at Winchester: though that is only a copy of the table that Merlin made in his fairy palace in the middle of the Valley of No Return.

CHAPTER SEVEN

THE SWORD IN THE GREAT WHITE STONE

gierne, as you know, was shut up in a castle, where Uther could never visit her, though he had loved her from a distance for a long time. But Merlin kept his promise, and, by his magic, made Uther able to take on the figure and voice of the lord of the castle, so that the King could come and go without anyone finding out. Merlin knew the future; he knew that Uther was destined to marry the lady Ygierne in the end. So he did not hesitate to help matters forward a little. When the lord of the castle was killed in battle, Uther Pendragon came to Ygierne in his own form. He told her that he loved her and would always protect her. So she married him and became his Queen.

After the marriage, King Uther Pendragon and his sweet and lovely lady Ygierne lived very happily in a castle called Tintagel by the Cornish Sea. You may see the ruins of it now, but you can never perhaps imagine how fine and strong it was in those days, hundreds of years ago. Folks were brave and cheerful then, and, though they certainly had terrible battles with other tribes, they were happy and courageous between times. The knights loved and fought for the fair ladies. And, bravest, most loving, and fairest of all, were King Uther Pendragon and Ygierne, the Queen.

Well, they were very happy together at Tintagel, and by and by, their little son was born. Ygierne knew, now, that Uther had promised to give the baby instantly into Merlin's charge. She was very sad about this, but she would not ask the King to break his word. Besides, she and Uther had often talked of the great future which Merlin had foretold for their child. So the King and Queen kissed the baby Prince, and the Queen herself wrapped him up in a beautiful cloak of cloth-of-gold and gave him into the charge of two ladies and two knights. Then Uther told the two ladies and the two knights to carry the tiny Prince to a certain little half-hidden door in the castle wall, to open this door softly and silently, and to give the child into the arms of somebody who would be waiting.

Singing little soft lullabies, the two ladies stepped carefully down the corridor, followed by the two knights. They reached the winding stairs and went down, down, down to the little half-hidden door. One lady carried the baby on a golden cushion, asleep in its golden cloak.

They opened the door, and the light of the candles which the two knights carried shone out into the dark, still night. From among the shadows came a dim tall figure. It held out its hands for the baby, and the ladies and the knights gave the tiny boy into the stranger's arms. Then they went back through the door and, as they climbed the winding staircase, they heard the distant trotting of a horse.

On the horse rode Merlin with the baby. Over hill and dale he went, until he reached a quiet small castle in a valley. Here lived a good and sober knight called Sir Hector, who knew well why Merlin had come. Long ago, the magician and King Uther had sent for Sir Hector and asked him if he would receive a little child into his house – a little child who was to become very great and famous, but who must be brought up simply as a noble knight's son. He had consented and had been given lands and riches in return. So, when Merlin rode up in the dark night, Sir Hector and his wife met the magician gladly and took the baby straight to their own nursery. Then Merlin had the little Prince christened "Arthur". Sir Hector brought him up in his own good, quiet, and happy home.

But Merlin was always at hand, watching over the boy. His father, King Uther, was content to leave little Arthur in the great wizard's charge. However, when he was dying, he sent for Merlin and asked for news of the child.

How happy he was when he heard that Prince

Arthur was growing up into a fine, strong boy. How much better it was, later, that he should have been brought up just as a good knight, instead of as a king's first-born son! Then Uther gave back the Round Table to Merlin and told him how it might be kept safe until Arthur came into his kingdom. Accordingly, Merlin had it carried far away to Cameliard, where it was placed in the care of an old friend of Uther's, another great King, whose name was Leodogran, who, in his turn, put it into the charge of two hundred and fifty knights, all of them brave, noble and good. What happened to it, afterwards, you will hear in another story.

So Uther died, but nobody knew that the little lad in Sir Hector's house was the dead King's son and heir. The barons of the country began to quarrel among themselves. Each of them wanted the power to rule over the rest. So at last, Merlin went to the Archbishop, who despaired over these things, and told him to call all the barons to London for Christmas, that they might go to service in the church and forget their quarrels, if only for the gentle hours of Christmas Day.

The barons dared not disobey the Archbishop, so to London and to church they duly went. The service over, out streamed the congregation into the church-yard. And there they saw something that had assuredly not been visible when they went in.

There in the eastern side of the churchyard, lit by the pale Christmas sun, stood a stone as white as marble. In the middle of it was a square of steel, and from the steel rose the glittering handle of a strong sharp sword. In letters of gold around the sword were written strange and thrilling words – words which said that whoever could draw the sword out of the stone was King of Britain, Uther Pendragon's only rightful heir.

The barons crowded around the stone, wide-eyed and amazed. Each called out that he, if given a chance, was certainly the one and only chieftain who could draw the sword from the stone. Smiling oddly, Merlin, who stood near, bade them all try. Jostling each other in their hurry, they sprang, one by one, to the side of the stone, seized the handle of the sword, and pulled and tugged with all their might. But their efforts were not a bit of good. The sword did not even tremble in its square of steel.

At last, the barons, tired and angry, left the churchyard and began to amuse themselves by holding a tournament in some meadows not very far away. After all, it was Christmas time – the season for junketings, jaunts, and knightly games. And, riding to the tournament as a matter of course came Sir Hector, his son Sir Kay, and the fair and noble boy Arthur, whom Sir Hector loved as much as his own child.

As they passed the churchyard, they saw the sword, shining in the stone that was like beautiful white marble, and they spoke to each other of the strangeness of the sight. Then they trotted on, and just as they were about to ride into the meadow, Sir Kay exclaimed, in dismay, that he could take no share in the tournament, for he had left his sword at home!

"Turn your horse quickly, my son," said Sir Hector to young Arthur. "Gallop home and fetch your brother's sword. *You* are too young for the knightly games, but *he* must on no account be left out of them."

Home Arthur went, full speed, to fetch his "brother's" sword. But, when he reached the house, everything was lonely and locked up. Sir Hector's lady had gone to the tournament herself, and had taken all the servants with her!

For a minute, Arthur hesitated. Then he was struck by the happiest thought. "I will go to the churchyard," said he, "and take the sword that is sticking out of the big white stone!"

So he mounted his horse again, and off to the churchyard he rode. Dismounting, he hastened to the great stone. There, not even pausing to read the words which were written in the golden letters, he took the sword by the handle and pulled. Lo and behold! the sword came easily and lightly from the steel in the middle of the marble.

Sword in hand, Arthur once more sprang into the saddle and galloped away to the tournament. Over the meadow grass he trotted, and straight into the hands of Sir Kay he gave the sword. Then, like the light-hearted modest boy he was, he fell back among the other youngsters, watching to see his elder brother's triumph.

But Sir Kay was staring at the sword. He turned it this way and that, then rode off to where his father watched.

"Sir," he said to Sir Hector, "this sword which young Arthur has brought me is the very sword that no baron could draw from the stone in the east of the churchyard! You have heard what was written around it in letters of gold?"

"I have heard," said Sir Hector, grave and start-led. For he, too, had been told the story of the sword set so firmly in the beautiful white stone! He, too, rec-ognized it now.

"If this is so, sir," cried Sir Kay, with a glowing face, "then I – I – must be King of Britain, Uther Pendragon's heir!"

But Sir Hector, deep in thought, had turned his horse's head. "Call your brother Arthur," he said. "And, both of you, follow me."

In silence, they rode to the churchyard. When they all dismounted near the stone, Sir Hector looked at

Arthur, who stood quietly by.

"Put the sword back again!" said he. And Arthur did so.

Sir Hector turned, then, to Sir Kay.

"Draw it out," he commanded. But Sir Kay could no more do this than any of the barons who had tried so hard.

Then Sir Hector himself tried and also failed. Tenderly, he laid his hand on Arthur's shoulder.

"It is your turn, now. Show me – show your brother – the truth!"

So Arthur, still quite simply and naturally, drew the sword for the second time and would have given it into Sir Hector's hand. But Sir Hector, instead of taking the sword, bent on one knee, and did Arthur homage, as all good knights do homage to their liege lord and King.

"My son," said he, "– and that I cannot help calling you, though you are not my son – the writing in the golden letters was set down on the marble slab for *you*! Hail! Arthur, son of Uther Pendragon, and King of Britain!"

CHAPTER EIGHT

A LADY OF THE LAKE

verybody in Britain knew that the only son of Uther Pendragon had been found at last; and, though some of the barons were very angry and refused at first to accept the "beardless boy," as they called him, they gave in when Queen Ygierne openly declared him to be the child of the dead King and herself. So Arthur was crowned with great rejoicings and feastings, jousts and tournaments.

Never was there so handsome and so special a young monarch! Not only did all the knights and ladies of his court think the world of him, but the fairies of the forests and lakes loved him, too. Had he not been given into the special care of Merlin, that master of magic, who knew a hundred times more secrets than the fairies knew themselves? Arthur's sister, too, was half a fairy, and was called Morgan-la-Fée, which means Morgan, the fairy maiden. She knew all sorts of spells, both good and bad. She could read stories in the stars and tell you the wonderful enchantments that might, on any moonlit night, be woven by means of a hazel wand, held in a certain, very secret, manner. She knew exactly what kind of fern seed would make you invisible, and where to find the flowers that were used for wonderful wine that smelled like cowslips and wild honey and made you fall head-over-heels in love! There was no end to Morgan-the-Fairy's magic.

Arthur and his sister were very fond of each other, though, like a good many other brothers and sisters, they quarrelled a little sometimes. It is, however, pretty certain that Morgan had something to do with the way in which the young King came into possession of a second sword, much more wonderful than the one which he had pulled out of the shining white stone.

Not very far from Arthur's castle – which was at a place called Caerleon, quite a long way from Tintagel – a big woods grew, all dark and shady with pines and oaks. In the middle of the woods was a fountain, which was always full of clear spring water. Beside the fountain, a beautiful tent appeared one day, hung inside with satin curtains and decorated with tassels of silver and gold. Just outside the tent, a horse in bright rich trappings was tethered; and, on a bough over the horse's head, hung a magnificent shield, set thickly with jewels, and enamelled in all the shades of a peacock's tail!

As soon as this lovely tent, and horse, and shield, appeared by the side of the fountain, all the passersby knew their meaning. Some strange and powerful knight from a distant country had taken up his post in the middle of one of King Arthur's private forests, and was challenging anybody and everybody to come and turn him out! This was a thing that happened very often in those days; and there was never any lack of knights to answer the challenge. It meant glory and renown to every knight who rode out to do him battle, and great distinction to the one who succeeded in conquering him.

The first person to come and tell Arthur about the knight was a very brave youth called Griflet, who was only a page at the court of Caerleon. He begged the King to give him the order of knighthood, that he might ride off at once and fight with the stranger, who, he said eagerly, was one of the strongest, bravest, cleverest knights in the whole world. Arthur hesitated, for he thought Griflet was too inexperienced and young. But Merlin told him to do as the lad asked; so the King made him a knight, calling him "Sir Griflet" and made him promise to come back to the court if he failed in the brave deed he was so anxious to perform. Sir Griflet promised and rode off. But, in a few hours, he came riding back, terribly wounded and dreadfully unhappy. The knight by the fountain had easily conquered him, but instead of killing him, the stranger had, himself, dismounted and given aid to poor Sir Griflet, telling him he was a brave youngster and would make a fine fighter when

Chapter Seven: The Sword in the Great White
Stone

The Sword came easily and lightly from
the steel in the middle of the marble when
the boy Arthur, and only he, drew it out.
His beloved adopted father, Sir Hector, led
the other knights in kneeling before their
new king, Arthur, son of Uther Pendragon.

Chapter Eight: A Lady of the Lake

When the strange knight saw the King riding in the forest, he stepped forward and stood, very proud and upright, barring the way that led on through the woods.

he was a little older. Then he had set the young knight on his horse again and sent him back to the King.

Well, when Arthur heard Sir Griflet's story, he exclaimed that the stranger was, indeed, a fine and generous knight, and that he would himself go off to the forest and challenge him to a battle! For, in those days, the more splendid and brave an enemy was, the more glory there was in fighting him. So off went King Arthur on a magnificent war-horse, his shield and sword and breastplate shining brightly.

On the way, Merlin walked by the King's stirrup, saying he thought he might be wanted before the day was over. As he and Arthur talked together, they came in sight of a richly-decorated tent, with the strange knight dressed in all his bright armour, standing by the side of the tree where his shield was hanging, its jewels and enamel gleaming in the shade of the boughs. When he saw another knight riding in the forest, he stepped forward and stood barring the way.

"How now!" cried Arthur. "Then no one may pass this way without a fight?"

"That is so," answered the knight, as bold and haughty as you please. "Are you ready?"

"Quite ready!" replied Arthur joyfully.

So the stranger leaped upon his horse, and, with sword and spear, King and knight sprang towards each other to do battle. Such a crash rang through the forest as they met! But the noise was only the noise of the King's spear striking the shield of the knight, and the knight's spear striking the shield of the King. And so vigorously each struck that both the spears were shivered into a thousand pieces.

By this time, both King and knight were hot with battle, and, springing from their horses, they rushed at each other on foot, brandishing their sharp, shining swords. Over and over again they struck, one at the other, each trying to strike the conquering blow. At last, the stranger-knight drew back for a moment. King Arthur, thinking he was exhausted, leaped towards him. But the other swung his sword suddenly high above his head and brought it with all his force against the King's sword as Arthur made his spring. So violent was the knight's great blow that it cut right through the sword of the King, who was left with only the jagged handle in his grasp.

Then Arthur threw away the handle and rushed at the knight with his mailed gloves. So they fought again, rocking and swaying together like two mighty wrestlers. And, at last, King Arthur was thrown to the ground and lay senseless among the bruised ferns.

The stranger-knight lifted high his own unbroken sword to cut off the fainting King's head. But Merlin, who had been watching, sprang forward and waved his wizard's wand. Instantly, the knight slipped slowly to the ground and lay beside the King in a deep sleep; while Merlin lifted Arthur and set him, only half-conscious, on the stranger's horse.

The King, pale and exhausted, looked down on the knight as Merlin led the horse away. "Oh, Merlin, Merlin!" he cried. "You have killed the finest knight that ever did battle against a King!"

"Not so!" answered Merlin. "He is only asleep! But come! You must have another sword to make up for the one that has been broken in the fight!"

So on they went, through the trees, with Merlin still leading the horse. Presently, they came to a big open space in the forest. There, in the afternoon sunlight, glimmered the wide waters of a mysterious lake. Nothing and nobody was in sight – no people, no wild foxes or deer. But, right in the middle of the lake, a white hand and arm were stretched out from the water, as motionless as if they were carved in ivory. A long sleeve of pearly satin was folded about the arm; and the hand held the most beautiful jewelled sword that Arthur had ever seen in his life.

As the King looked, amazed, he saw a fairy maiden in a silver gown, with golden hair, walking on the green water. She came stepping daintily towards them, and Arthur asked Merlin who she was. "She is Nimue, the Lady of the Lake," said Merlin, "and, if you ask her, very courteously, she will tell you how to get the sword." So, when the Lady of the Lake set her pretty little foot on the shore, Arthur went towards her and, bowing low, asked her to tell him how he could get the sword.

Then the maiden smiled and showed him a fairy barge hidden among the reeds. She told him he had only to get into the barge, and to row himself into the middle of the lake, and to take the sword out of the fair white hand which held it. "And for my reward for telling you," said she, "one day I will come to the court and claim a special kindness from you!" Then she disappeared, and Arthur and Merlin, springing into the barge, rowed out as fast as they could.

All this time, the hand and arm that held the sword had remained quite still. Arthur looked in amazement as he drew nearer and nearer, at the slim wrist and the delicate fingers of that white strange hand!

The barge drew close up to the motionless arm; Arthur, leaning over the side, put out his hand. Very gently and carefully, he drew the shining sword from the fairy fingers. As soon as he touched it, they released their clasp, and the arm went slowly, slowly down into the lake and was gone.

Then Merlin rowed the barge back again to the rocky, reedy bank of the lake. The lady who had told them to take the sword had disappeared among the dark pines that grew right down to the water's edge.

Arthur and Merlin got out of the barge, and Arthur fastened the fairy sword to his side. Then Merlin, who had read all about it in one of his fairy books, told him that the sword was called "Excalibur," and that it was just as precious and wonderful as the Round Table itself. The wizard told the King, too, the name of the stranger-knight, which was Pellinore, and said that he, also, was a great King. But, when Arthur wanted to go and finish the battle with Pellinore – now that he had a fairy sword – Merlin said that he had fought enough for one day. So he and the King rode back to Caerleon with Excalibur hanging by Arthur's side, while King Pellinore awoke quietly from his enchanted sleep and went to rest in his tent.

CHAPTER NINE

THE PRINCESS GUINEVERE

ing Leodogran, as you know, was the old friend of King Uther Pendragon, who had been given the task of looking after Merlin's wonderful Round Table. The Round Table was kept in the banqueting hall of Leodogran's big stone castle at Cameliard. All the knights who feasted there were under a vow; and the words of this vow were some of the noblest words that have ever been spoken in the history of the world. In addition to the Round Table, Leodogran's castle held another great treasure – his only daughter Guinevere, the most beautiful and gracious maiden in the whole wide earth.

Guinevere flitted about the castle like a fairy princess, so golden was her hair, so blue were her eyes, so peach-pink her delicate cheeks. When her father's step was heard on the flagstones of the castle floors, Guinevere would lay everything aside and hasten to meet and look after him.

One morning, the King of Cameliard, who had been away for some days, came galloping back to the castle on his war-horse and cried to the servants to let down the portcullis – the great entrance door – to raise the bridge over the moat, and to prepare for a siege. His enemies were riding in hundreds over the near hills. The Knights of the Round Table came hurrying into the great hall; their pages ran after them to buckle on each master's armour. But, instead of a page, Leodogran was waited upon by his own daughter, the Princess Guinevere. Praying to heaven to protect him, she watched the King ride out at the head of his noble knights. Then she, herself, looked after the preparations for the siege of the castle before, running lightly up the winding stone stairs, she took up her stand by the window of a high tower, from which she could watch the battle.

What a clash of armies she saw outside! Here, there, and everywhere flashed Leodogran in his bright breastplate, supported always by the knights of the Round Table. For a long while, they held their own, but by and by Princess Guinevere felt her heart shaken with sudden fear. She saw the knights pressed hard on every side by an army stronger in numbers than themselves. They were being driven back towards the castle walls.

Princess Guinevere went numb and cold with dismay. Then, all at once, she heard a shout of encouragement and triumph. Down among her father's foes came riding an unknown knight, the noblest in bearing that the Princess had ever seen. Above his head floated a banner which showed a Dragon wrought in gleaming gold! In his hand shone a sword of brilliant steel, its handle set thickly with diamonds, rubies, and pearls.

In and out, backwards and forwards, glittered the golden sign of the Dragon, while the strange knight's sword flashed among the enemy like a flame. He had slain hundreds of Leodogran's enemies, when, quite suddenly, an old man appeared by his bridle and threw his war-horse back upon its haunches.

"Enough!" cried this old man, "Enough! Do you not see that the battle is won?"

The stranger-knight paused and slowly pushed his sword into its sheath. Then up rode King Leodogran, grim, blood-stained, and weary. He bent low in his saddle.

"Beautiful and courageous knight!" said Leodogran. "How can I thank you? Come – follow me into my castle. I do not know who you are, but you have saved my home for me, and anything in it is yours for the asking."

Then the big portcullis was raised again, the bridge let down over the moat. Two and two, kings and knights, they all rode into the courtyard of the castle.

How busy everybody in the castle was, to be sure! Pages, with big baskets on their arms, were covering the floors with bright fresh rushes. Cooks in the kitchen were roasting and stewing and baking. And delighted smiling maidens were pouring cool scented water into basins, taking clean white towels from the shelves and bringing soft rich robes into the big hall, ready to lay on the knights' shoulders when the pages had taken off the stained and heavy armour.

King Leodogran led the stranger-knight to the seat of honour and bade him rest. As the tired soldier sank down upon a couch of sweet-smelling rushes, he saw a lovely lady coming forward from among the sewing-maidens who were waiting on the knights. She wore the prettiest gold head-dress, the daintiest silk gown in the world, and she carried her silver basin and white towel very carefully indeed. It was the Princess Guinevere, hastening to wait, courteously and lovingly, on her father, the King.

But, as she curtseyed deeply to him, he waved her from him and pointed to his guest. "Wait, first, on the stranger-knight," said Leodogran. "Had it not been for his help, the castle of Cameliard would have fallen."

So Guinevere turned from her father to the stranger-knight. And, the moment the eyes of the knight and the maiden met, the two fell in love!

How wonderful it seemed to both! The soldier in his battle-dress looked adoringly at the sweet face under the golden head-dress. Guinevere, for her part, hardly lifted her shy blue eyes from the ground as she tended the stranger. The old man, who had entered the castle with the knights, smiled as he watched them and, drawing near to Leodogran, pointed out the pretty sight.

"You offered anything your castle held, to your deliverer," said he. "I think I know what gift your visitor will be asking!"

King Leodogran started, and looked dismayed. "Who is he?" he asked. "And who, old man, are you?"

The King stared very closely at his unknown visitor.

"No matter – no matter!" said he. "But what of your promise to give the knight anything he asks?"

"My promise shall be kept," said Leodogran proudly. And the old man smiled again.

Then everyone in the hall began to move towards the banqueting room, and the two hundred and fifty knights took their places at the Round Table, which was spread for a great feast. King Leodogran stood watching them; and the stranger-knight stepped forward and joined him, looking at him very earnestly.

"Good and great King," said he, "I am from a distant court and do not know your customs. What is this Round Table, and who are these knights who have taken their places about it?"

Leodogran answered gravely:

"Brave stranger," he said, "that Round Table was left in my charge by a great King – Uther Pendragon himself. Whoever takes his place at it must share in a noble vow. Will you sit among my two hundred and fifty knights? Will you join in the words of the vow?"

The knight's face had become very bright and eager when he heard the name of Uther Pendragon. He made a quick step forward and took his seat at the table.

"Will you admit me to your fellowship?" he cried in a piercing voice.

Then all the two hundred and fifty knights sprang to their feet, and two hundred and fifty voices rang out in the great vow.

"To right the wrong, to punish the guilty, to feed the hungry, to help the feeble, to obey the law, and never to turn away from a woman in distress; this is the vow of the Knights of the Round Table!"

The sound of voices ceased, and everybody turned to the stranger, who had drawn his sword, and was holding it on high. Word for word, he repeated the vow in a ringing voice.

Leodogran stepped forward, and held up his hand for silence.

"Sir Knight," he said, "who are you?"

With a triumphant smile, the stranger answered:

"I am Arthur, King of Britain, and proud to have become a Knight of the Round Table –"

He paused for a moment, then moved swiftly forward and knelt, on one knee, before Guinevere:

"And prouder still, King Leodogran, to put my sword, my spear, my life, at the service of this fair and beautiful lady!"

Then the old man came towards them, and King Leodogran knew him for Merlin, the great magician. Merlin took Guinevere's hand and held it towards her father; and Leodogran placed it in Arthur's quick clasp, and, raising him to his feet, bent very low before him.

"My liege and lord," said he, "I would have given my daughter gladly to the knight who saved Cameliard. How much more joyfully I give her to Arthur, son of Uther Pendragon, King of Britain, and Knight of the Round Table."

CHAPTER TEN

THE EMPTY SEAT AT THE ROUND TABLE

ne spring morning, the sun rose, bright and beautiful, over the high towers of Camelot. The birds were singing among the apple-bloom; the may-blossoms were nodding their heads among the long grass. Camelot was hung with banners and flags; its pathways were arched with rainbows of flowers. Magnificent tapestries adorned the walls; fresh rushes, mixed with garlands, covered the stone floors. Everybody was running about with silver dishes and golden goblets, with cakes and fruit and honey and wine. For King Arthur's wedding day was close at hand, and Guinevere was on her way to Camelot with a train of ladies-in-waiting and a bodyguard of knights, bringing the Round Table that had been made by Merlin.

At this Round Table, as you know, the young King had taken his knightly vow. How glad he was to think that it was to stand under the roof of Camelot, and that, sitting all around it, his fellow-knights would join in his wedding breakfast. He stood with Merlin in the great gateway of his royal castle, dressed in armour that shone like gold. On all sides were his faithful courtiers, waiting to greet the strangers who were coming from the court of Leodogran. The great company of the Round Table was to be completed today. Many knights had made the vow in times gone by; some had been killed in battle. But today, the day before Arthur's wedding, every seat was to be filled.

This was the King's purpose, as he waited at the entrance of his castle in his suit of gold. Presently, from the distance, came the murmur of a crowd, the tramping of horses' feet, and the roll of wheels. Over the hills towards Camelot poured the glittering procession of the royal bride – banners waving, and minstrels singing stirring and noble songs. It was a magnificent sight.

King Arthur's heart was beating fast with excitement and joy as the procession came right up to the big castle gates. He moved forward and bent very, very low. For, on the leading horse, he saw his lovely lady, Guinevere, riding in royal dignity. Close behind her rode her pages. Then came her ladies-in-waiting, each with a handsome knight in attendance. In the very midst of the procession marched a tall old man in white, crowned with mistletoe and singing songs to the sound of a harp which he held in his hands; while a number of men followed just behind, carrying the Round Table!

King Arthur stepped forward and lifted Guinevere from her horse. Who knows what he did not whisper

Chapter Eight: A Lady of the Lake

A white hand and arm were stretched out
from the water. In it was the most beautiful
sword Arthur had ever seen
in his life.

Chapter Nine: The Princess Guinevere

The beautiful Princess brought cool, clear water in a silver bowl to wait upon her father, King Leodogran. The moment that the stranger-knight's eyes met hers, the two fell in love.

to her before he set her on the ground? Then he took her hand and led her forward, across the courtyard, between rows and rows of smiling, bowing attendants, right into the castle of Camelot, with the knights and ladies, who had come with her from her father's court, walking two-and-two behind.

A beautiful throne had been set high on a dais for the Princess, and Arthur led her up to it. He watched her seat herself before he turned to welcome the noble company who followed. He bowed over the hands of the fair ladies; and all the knights bent, with stately courtesy, in greeting. The Round Table was brought in and put in the very middle of the hall. Arthur drew near and watched while his servants placed the seats around it. When they had set as many as it would hold, the King called his knights to gather round.

From among the brilliant company in the hall, a hundred knights stepped forward, all of whom had come with Princess Guinevere from the court of her father, King Leodogran. As they approached the Round Table, Arthur counted them over, one by one. When the hundred were complete, the King bowed to them once more. Then he turned to Merlin, who again stood beside him. Merlin took a roll of parchment from his pocket and began to read from it.

He was reading the names of those among Arthur's own knights who had, for their courage and their goodness, their truth, charity, and uprightness, been considered worthy to join the noble fellowship of the Round Table. Some were old and scarred with battle; some were middle-aged; some were quite young, keen and anxious to fight for glory and for the King. When the names echoed down the hall, they stepped forward, one by one. Bowing to Princess Guinevere as they passed the high dais, and to King Arthur as they reached him where he stood, they joined the hundred knights from the court of King Leodogran. Then the chief butler came forward with a great jewelled goblet in his hand, followed by two pages carrying golden jugs. The knights and the King took their seats at the table. The goblet was filled, and, passing the jewelled cup from hand to hand, everybody drank to the fellowship of knights.

All this time, Guinevere watched, smiling and gracious, from her throne on the high dais. The knights looked at each other, and at the King, as they drank from the glittering cup; but they all rose to their feet and looked towards their future Queen, on her throne in the midst of them, as, at a sign from Arthur, their voices rang out, loud and glad and brave, in the words of the great vow.

The sound died away; now it was the Princess Guinevere's turn to rise to her feet, sweet and fair and royal among them all. How proud and happy the King must have felt when he saw his lady standing among these bright and starry gentlemen, accepting their promise of chivalry with so delicate a grace! She curtseyed very low to them all and waved her pretty white hands. Then she sat down again among her ladies; and, one by one, the knights of the Round Table stepped forward, and, kneeling on one knee before Arthur, took the oath of loyalty to the King.

Merlin stood by, his roll of parchment, folded neatly up again, in his hand. As each knight made his vow, the wizard bent his grave wise head. But, all the time, he seemed as if in a dream.

Then, while he looked at the Round Table, he saw a mysterious thing happen. On all the seats that were placed around it, letters of gold began to appear. They looked as if they were being written by invisible fingers holding an invisible pen. As Merlin watched, these letters grew bigger and brighter. The old magician moved forward to read them more clearly. When he stood quite close to the table, the wonder on his face changed into great gladness.

For what do you think had been written, in each seat, by the invisible fingers that held the invisible pen? Why, the name of the knight who had just risen from it to do homage to King Arthur, chief of them all. It was a sure sign to Merlin that the Round Table had been made, by his own hands, for these very knights, and that their names were written also around the Silver Table which had been lost to men. He called to the King and to the knights to come and read. They all gathered round, amazed, and spelled out the letters of their names. Then they took their places, shoulder to shoulder. But, even as they did so, they saw that every seat was not yet filled. Two of them, one on Arthur's right hand, the other on his left, were still empty and un-named.

Then King Arthur was very grieved and disappointed, for he had hoped that, today, the Fellowship of the Round Table would be quite complete. But Merlin had, all at once, seen into the future, and he knew the secret of those two empty seats. He laid his hand on the King's shoulder and consoled him.

"Be patient," said the magician, "be patient! In one empty seat, you will very soon see someone whom you know and admire already. In the other, the Seat Perilous, no knight may sit today, nor tomorrow, nor for many years to come. Look! See what is written there instead of a name."

Arthur looked, and lo! he saw letters appear at the second empty seat, written, not in gold, but in flame! Amazed, he read the words: "I am the Seat Perilous."

Even as he finished reading the words, they faded away. But all the knights had seen the letters of flame. And, right down the court, ran a murmur.

"That empty seat is the Seat Perilous, and no knight may sit in it today, or tomorrow, or for many years to come!"

CHAPTER ELEVEN
THE FAIRY HUNT

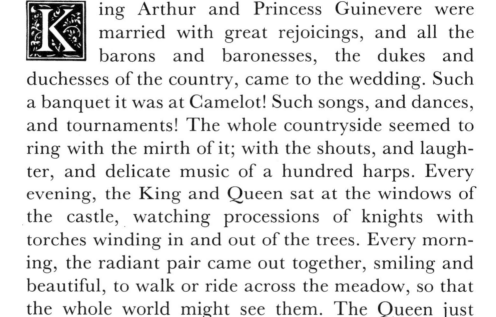

King Arthur and Princess Guinevere were married with great rejoicings, and all the barons and baronesses, the dukes and duchesses of the country, came to the wedding. Such a banquet it was at Camelot! Such songs, and dances, and tournaments! The whole countryside seemed to ring with the mirth of it; with the shouts, and laughter, and delicate music of a hundred harps. Every evening, the King and Queen sat at the windows of the castle, watching processions of knights with torches winding in and out of the trees. Every morning, the radiant pair came out together, smiling and beautiful, to walk or ride across the meadow, so that the whole world might see them. The Queen just moved along daintily and silently, but the King was always watchful and alert, ready to hear grievances or to grant requests: ready, even, to give the order of knighthood to the poor sons of workers and cowherds if they could prove to him that they were as noble and valiant at heart as any gentlemen of the land.

But a day came when Merlin told Arthur that the merriment and feasting must pause for a time, and that the King must meet his knights in sober and earnest talk, seated at the Round Table. So Queen Guinevere and all the ladies of the court swept and rustled away, in a stately procession, to the women's quarters in the castle; and the King and the knights sat down at the Round Table and passed the cup of fellowship from hand to hand. Then Merlin said that today the empty seat at the King's left hand was to be filled – not the Seat Perilous, but the other place which had been left without a name. Everyone wondered who the chosen knight could be; they all stood up and waited as the great wizard went out of the door of the banqueting hall to bring in the newcomer, and to present him to the King.

After a minute or two, the sound of a galloping horse was heard through the window – a strong, fast horse which came, with hoofs like thunder, over the drawbridge of the moat. A knight's shield clashed in the courtyard; a knight's small silken banner fluttered against the casement; Merlin's voice spoke a greeting; and deep full happy tones echoed in reply. Down the corridor tramped the heavy feet of the stranger, and in the doorway his form showed, tall and broad. Merlin took his hand and led him forward, and King Arthur gave a cry of amazement. For whom do you think it was? Why, none other than King Pellinore, the knight who had set up his tent by the side of the woodland fountain, and who had been left lying in an enchanted sleep the last time that

Arthur had seen him!

But King Arthur was pleased – oh, very pleased indeed! He bore the other King no ill-will for having broken his own royal sword – and very nearly his own royal head as well – in their mighty battle among the forest trees. Stepping forward, he greeted his old enemy warmly, declaring that he was a right goodly and noble knight, worthy to become a member of the Round Table. Pellinore said, in reply, that he was proud of many things in his life, but never prouder than at this moment, when he stood in the halls of Camelot and received the greeting of Camelot's King. Then he bent on one knee before Arthur and took the oath of fealty; and Arthur, himself, raised him up and placed him in the seat at his left-hand side, while the jewelled cup was passed around again, and all the other knights drank joyfully to Pellinore, the latest arrival at the Round Table.

And now Merlin made a sign to Arthur, and the King sprang to his feet and drew his sword from his scabbard. Everybody else did the same. There was a moment's pause, and then all the brave voices rang out together. Standing side by side, shoulder to shoulder, their unsheathed swords glittering, their heads high and erect, the knights of the Round Table thundered out the words of the Vow.

The sound of it was still in the air, and not one of the company had sheathed his sword again, when a great commotion arose under the windows of the castle! Hounds were baying, horns were blowing, and a little dog seemed to be barking with all its might! A long, long way off, horses might be heard galloping as well. But nobody could be quite sure of that, because, as they all stared at each other in great astonishment, the door of the banqueting hall suddenly burst open, and a huge, pure-white stag, with branching horns and eyes like balls of flame, bounded into the room, its hoofs, which seemed to be made of silver, flashing and ringing among the green rushes on the stone flags of the floor.

No sooner had it leapt through the doorway than everybody saw that the little white dog, which had been making such a noise outside, was hard on the heels of this beautiful and mysterious deer. And, following instantly, came a pack of thirty pairs of great black hounds, in full cry after the snow-white stag. But of followers and huntsmen there was not a sign. Only the sound of fairy horns blowing in the air, and the galloping of unseen horses far away.

Around the big banqueting hall swept this strange hunt, which was, in very truth, a hunt from Fairyland. Just as the great white stag reached the place where a young handsome knight was sitting, the little dog sprang right up at it, so that the big beautiful creature leapt almost over the young knight's head. This knight was called Sir Gawaine, and the stag knocked him clean over. Sir Gawaine sprang up, quite bewitched, and, catching up the little dog, joined the hunt, not knowing that it was a fairy hunt and would lead him goodness knows whither! Away he ran out of the room and out of the castle, and, putting the little dog on his horse just as huntsmen always did, went galloping off after the snow-white stag. But no sooner was he out of the door than a beautiful maiden, on the prettiest white pony, came in at another. She rode right into the middle of the hall and called to King Arthur to go after Sir Gawaine and to bring back the little fairy dog which he had stolen!

"The little dog is mine!" cried this beautiful unknown lady. "The knight had no business to take it away! Remember the Vow, King Arthur, remember the Vow! I am a lady in distress, and, as such, you have sworn to help me!"

King Arthur sat silent, his hand on his sword. The Vow had seemed to him such a beautiful serious thing, and he could not believe that it had anything to do with this wild fairy hunt, or this strange fairy lady, who certainly was not made of flesh and blood. He heard the noise of the black hounds, and of Sir Gawaine's horse, and of the little mysterious elfin dog, fade in the distance among the faintly-blowing horns of the invisible company; and he had not the slightest wish to go after them. He wanted to stay soberly in his royal castle with his beautiful royal bride.

As he hesitated, another startling and quite unexpected visitor came loudly in through the wide-open door. This time, it was a strange, shadowy knight almost as big as a giant, dressed in black armour and riding a huge black horse. He trotted up to the lady, and, without a word to anybody, seized her pretty white pony by the bridle. Then he wheeled his horse around and rode quickly out of the door again, leading the lady's pony, and taking no notice of her cries and tears. It all happened so quickly that not a single knight of the Round Table had time to spring to the lady's rescue.

As they all stood, breathless and amazed, King Arthur suddenly found his voice and cried aloud, in ringing tones, to Merlin, the magician:

"Tell me, O great wizard," he cried, "what is the meaning of all this magic?"

Merlin, whose face had been hidden under his magician's hood, suddenly flung away the covering. Everybody saw him, for a moment, as an old man, with a long white beard, wearing a crown of mistletoe. But, even as they looked, his face changed. He seemed young and very beautiful, and the crown of mistletoe became a laurel wreath on his hair, which was golden and like a boy's. His voice, when he answered Arthur, somehow reminded the King of the invisible fairy horns which they had all heard.

"And what if the hunt is only a fairy hunt and the lady only a fairy lady?" cried Merlin, "Are you not brave enough to follow them into Fairyland? Is all your life going to be spent in royal castles, eating and drinking at rich banquets, and meeting other knights in mock battles, with swords and shields? Do you not know what high adventure means? If not, I can soon tell you! It means the adventure of bright dreams, and of lovely visions, and of things that are only very dimly seen and heard. Follow the Fairy Hunt, good King Arthur! Go after the vision of the snow-white stag, and the sweet sorrowful lady, and the dark knight! What if she has only asked you to bring back her little white dog? What if you think it is all magic mixed with folly, and you would be better staying quietly at home? Have the kingly courage to take horse and to follow Sir Gawaine into Fairyland – to storm the doors of the Castle Perilous and to brave the darkness of the Valley of No Return!"

Then Arthur drew himself erect, and King Pellinore sprang to his feet at the King's right hand. "I, too, am a King," cried Pellinore. "I, too, am of royal blood! It is for kings to lead the way into the mysterious places of which the great wizard has spoken. Come, King Arthur! We will set off on this high adventure together!"

"You say well!" cried Merlin. "You have your own

good sword, King Pellinore! You have used it well and strongly more than once. Use it well and strongly again! And for you, my own great sovereign, you have Excalibur! Excalibur, which you took from the hand that held it high above the enchanted lake! Carry Excalibur with you, and use it, always, to defend the right. Then you need not fear the places of dark spirits! Forward, forward, both of you! Go, like brave and chivalrous Kings, into Fairyland!"

Merlin finished speaking and folded his hood once more about his face and hair. King Arthur and King Pellinore went out of the banqueting hall and sprang each upon his own war-horse. Then off they went, side by side, after the Fairy Hunt, while Merlin, hidden in his hood, passed away from the sight of the knights of the Round Table. Where he went, none of them knew.

CHAPTER TWELVE
KING PELLINORE'S ADVENTURE

ing Pellinore had many adventures in his day, but the one you are going to hear about was the greatest of all. You remember that he had galloped off at full speed after the Fairy Hunt. He swore to himself that he would save the pretty weeping lady who had been carried off by the Black Knight, or wander in the Enchanted Forest for the rest of his life. He had become separated from King Arthur and was quite alone among the trees; but, just in front of him, he could still hear the baying of the sixty coal-black hounds.

He rode on as fast as he could, and then something happened. The baying of the hounds suddenly went all muffled and strange, as if they had disappeared inside a cave. The King turned the corner; and there, in front of him, stood a great beast. It was not like a lion, nor a bear, nor even a dragon, nor anything in the world except itself. It stood and glared at him, before turning around and lumbering away, crashing through the undergrowth with as much noise as a hippopotamus. And, through the mouth of the beast, there still came the muffled baying of the hounds.

This strange monster had swallowed them all, but they seemed still to be hunting the fairy stag in the very inside of the beast!

King Pellinore gave a great shout, for he had been hunting this beast all his life, and he knew he would probably go on hunting it until he died and never be able to kill it! But, meanwhile, he followed it hard through bush and briar. At last, the beast disappeared altogether, and he saw a lady sitting by a fountain. She showed him the path through the Enchanted Forest that he must take and told him that already the Black Knight and the pretty weeping maiden had gone that way.

He heard the hounds still baying, but a long, long way off, as he hurried down the path the lady had shown him. In a very few minutes, he reached a clearing in the wood, where two beautiful tents, one blue and one crimson, were set up opposite each other in the shadows of the trees. At the door of one of these tents stood the maiden he had come to save; and, on the trodden grass in the middle of the clearing, the Black Knight, on the black horse, was doing battle, with sword and shield, against another knight who seemed almost as big and strong as his enemy.

King Pellinore poised his spear in his raised hand and, galloping forward, drove his way between them. "How, now?" he cried. "How is this? Who are you both, that you fight in this way for the lady yonder,

Chapter Ten: The Empty Seat at the Round Table

A procession of knights with torches
glittered through the forest. The royal
bride rode at its head in regal dignity, with
her pages and her ladies-in-waiting close
behind. It was a magnificent sight!

Chapter Ten: The Empty Seat at the Round Table

The knights all rose to their feet and looked
toward the dais on which stood their
beautiful future Quéen. At a sign from the
King, they raised their swords, and their
voices rang out, loud and glad and brave,
in the words of their great vow.

who belongs to neither of you, but come, of her own will, to ask the protection of King Arthur?"

"The lady is mine!" cried the Black Knight. "This foolish fellow, here, is trying to steal her from me. But she is mine! I fought King Arthur for her, and I conquered him!"

"That is not true!" shouted King Pellinore – and his voice rang all through the forest in its anger – "I was there and I saw it all! You carried the lady away before a single knight of the Round Table had time to spring to arms and do battle for her! I have followed the coal-black hounds, and the beast which swallowed the hounds, all the way through this Enchanted Forest to take the lady back again! Come! Meet me, here, in this open space of grass, and we will soon see which is the better man."

Then the Black Knight rushed upon King Pellinore, and with their swords and shields and spears, they fought until the forest rang with the noise. But the King was soon the conqueror. He killed the Black Knight's horse, and, when he saw his enemy lying on the crushed turf, he also sprang to the ground, to finish the fight fairly on foot. And finish it he did.

Then the other knight, who had watched the battle from a little distance, came forward gladly and told King Pellinore to take the lady back to Arthur's court. "I was but trying to save her from the Black Knight," he said. "I knew that he had no right to her!" And he brought out a fresh, strong horse that had been tethered to a tree. He put King Pellinore's saddle and bridle upon it and said he would care for the tired horse which had been in the battle. After that, he went up to the door of the tent and, giving his hand to the lady, led her forward.

The lady had stopped crying now and had let down her long veil and wound her hood about her head, so that King Pellinore could not see her face. He lifted her into the saddle before springing up in front of her. He thought that she felt like a sweet, small, cool thing, and that she smelled of wild roses and violets washed in dew. How lightly she seemed to sit behind him, too! His big horse took no account of her extra weight, as it trotted off through the trees, where the night shadows were gathering.

On and on rode King Pellinore and the lady, until it was quite dark. Then he stopped his horse and lifted her down, and they slept under the trees. He was almost surprised to see in the morning that she was still there, because he guessed she was more than half a fairy. When the sun was high in the sky, both King and lady rode safely into the courtyard of the castle at Camelot.

Then King Arthur, and Sir Gawaine (who, having soon lost the sound of the Fairy Hunt, had returned) and all the rest, came out to meet them. They welcomed the lady gladly, and gave praise and homage to King Pellinore. But the lady was still veiled; and, at last, King Arthur turned to her with courtesy.

"You will find shelter and happiness forever at my court," said he. "The knights of the Round Table will be at your service, always – ready to protect you, and never failing to respect you. But you came and went almost as swiftly, and with as much surprise to us, as the Fairy Hunt itself. Will you, then, let us now see your face?"

Then the lady threw back her veil and hood, and showed her pretty face to the King and all his knights. The knights murmured in admiration, for she was very beautiful. But the King cried out with joy, for he knew her now.

"You are sweet Nimue!" he exclaimed. "You are she who showed me the barge in which I rowed to take my sword Excalibur from the hand that held it above the water! You are one of those wonderful beings who love the world of knighthood – one of the Ladies of the Lake!"

"Yes, I am Nimue, a Lady of the Lake!" said she. "And you have fulfilled your promise to me, King Arthur! From today, I shall never be far away from you. With the other ladies, my fairy friends, I will come and go between the Enchanted Forest and the royal and knightly court at Camelot."

CHAPTER THIRTEEN

SIR GAWAINE'S ADVENTURE

ir Gawaine's most wonderful adventure of all came about through another knight, Sir Kay, who told a story of a hidden fountain which, he said, was to be found over the waters of the sea, in the heart of another enchanted forest, called Broceliande. There were strange tales related of this fountain – of its magical waters and the mysterious white marble slab upon its brink. Whoever could make way to the fountain would be sure of the finest adventure in all the world.

When Sir Gawaine heard about the fountain, and the promised adventure, he did not hesitate a moment. He sailed to Brittany, and took his horse and his shield with him. When he landed, he mounted and rode away over the moors and through the villages until he reached Broceliande. The enchanted part began in a valley, which was the loveliest valley in the world. A sparkling stream splashed and bubbled among the sunlit stones. Sir Gawaine followed the stream until he reached a castle which shone like silver. Two beautiful boys stood at the door of this castle, dressed in yellow satin with gold crowns on their heads and gold shoes on their feet. When the sound of Sir Gawaine's horse was heard in the castle windows, a tall man, also dressed in yellow satin, came out of the door and went out to meet the visitor.

The man in the shining robe led Sir Gawaine into the castle, where twenty-four maidens sat in a row. Six of them took Sir Gawaine's horse, six carried off his armour to wash it, and six took away his travel-stained clothes and brought him a robe, silk-lined, shining, and soft. The remaining six waited on him with silver bowls of clear water and fine damask towels. Then they spread a delicious feast for him, and the man in yellow satin asked where he was going.

When Sir Gawaine replied that he was going to the magical fountain in search of high adventure, the man in yellow satin seemed delighted to have met so brave a knight. He ordered Sir Gawaine's horse to be brought around and showed him the path that would take him where he wished to go. Sir Gawaine rode off and presently came to a sheltered glade, with a mound in the middle of it, where there sat an enormous black man with only one eye, set in the middle of his forehead. In his right hand, he held an iron club.

Around this great black giant stood a thousand wild animals – stags and boars, lions and tigers, serpents and dragons! Sir Gawaine was very much startled, but he spurred his horse on through the crowd of fierce growling beasts and, riding straight up to the one-eyed black giant, asked him boldly the way to the fairy fountain where a wandering knight could find the highest of high adventures.

The great black giant scowled at him with his one eye, but answered. If Sir Gawaine would ride a little farther down the valley, he would see, presently, the tallest, greenest tree he had ever seen in his life. Under this tree bubbled the fountain; by the side of the water, was a white marble slab. On the slab was set a bowl of silver, fastened with silver chain. Any knight who was brave enough to fill the silver bowl with water from the fountain, and then to pour the water over the white marble slab, would find himself in the middle of an adventure dangerous enough to satisfy the most courageous man.

All this the giant growled out unwillingly. Sir Gawaine was not sorry to leave, and he rode forward among the shady oaks and pines. Presently, he saw the tall and beautiful green tree of which the great giant had spoken – and there, at its foot were the white marble slab, the silver bowl, and the fairy fountain.

Sir Gawaine dismounted, and, without a moment's hesitation, took the silver bowl, filled it with water, and poured the water right over the white marble. In an instant, almost before he could spring on his horse again, the sky went as black as night, a clap of thunder shook the valley, and a hailstorm came beating and rattling about the tall green tree. Every leaf of the tree was beaten off, and then the storm passed, and the sun came out again. And behold! instead of putting out fresh leaves, the tall tree seemed to blossom into hundreds and hundreds of little birds, which set to singing more sweetly and exquisitely than the sweetest, most exquisite music Sir Gawaine had ever heard!

Then, as he sat on his horse, entranced, a loud deep wailing was heard along the valley and down through the sunlight galloped a knight, who was the blackest of all the black knights ever seen. And he rushed upon Sir Gawaine, who spurred his horse to meet the other, with a loud, defiant cry.

For many minutes, they fought beside the fairy fountain, and then Sir Gawaine gave the Black Knight a mortal blow. But he did not fall at once – he only turned his horse's head and galloped away, with Sir Gawaine after him. In a short time, the high walls of a palace showed through the trees. The Black Knight galloped across the drawbridge and through the lifted iron gate. But, when Sir Gawaine would have followed, the great gate slid down between the high walls again and shut him out.

Sir Gawaine, disappointed, got down from his horse and peeped through the bars. And, to his surprise, he met the gaze of a charming maiden with curly golden hair who, as he was peeping in, was, in the same way, peeping out!

"Who are you?" said she. "And what do you want?"

"I want to come inside!" cried Sir Gawaine.

The maiden nodded her head quite kindly.

"I have been waiting here for you a long time," said she. "But I cannot let you in for all the world to see! Take this ring. Put it on your finger, and you will be invisible, and then I will lift up the gate!"

So Sir Gawaine put on the ring and became invisible, and she lifted up the gate and admitted him. The maiden led him to a wonderful gilded and painted chamber and gave him a delicious supper. When he had finished, she bade him listen to sounds of wailing coming up from below.

"The lord of the castle is dead!" said she. "He was the Black Knight of the Fountain. But it was always told that his lady should marry one of Arthur's knights. You must be he."

"Yes, I must be he!" cried Sir Gawaine. "This is my high adventure, I know. Fair maiden, let me see the lady!"

"Peep through that little grating, and you will see her in the hall below," said the maiden.

So Sir Gawaine peeped, and, down in the hall, in a lovely black-and-silver gown, he saw a most beautiful lady sitting with candles all about her. She was pale and grave, but not very sad. She had never really loved the lord of the castle, but had, long ago, married him so that he might defend the fairy fountain. Her name had always been the Lady of the Fountain, and she knew that she must marry again, immediately, so that those magical waters, that white slab with the silver bowl, that tall green tree, might still be kept unhurt in the secret fairy places of Broceliande.

Sir Gawaine, watching her, felt his love for her spring up like a flame. He turned to the maiden in the page's dress.

"I love the Lady of the Fountain!" he cried. "I have always loved her in my dreams! Take me to her."

"Tomorrow!" said the maiden. "I will take you tomorrow. Be assured, she will love you in return!"

So, the next day, the maiden gave Sir Gawaine a beautiful robe to wear, with golden clasps in the shapes of lions. He looked royal in it as he strode down the corridors of the castle into the presence of the Lady of the Fountain, who was sitting thoughtful and all alone. The maiden led Sir Gawaine to her, and she turned her beautiful pale face to him, as he knelt, silently, on one knee before her.

"You?" she said. "Then it was you who fought with the Black Knight of the Fountain."

"It was my adventure, lady," said Sir Gawaine.

The Lady of the Fountain made a sign to the pretty maiden who was dressed like a page.

"Call my nobles," said she.

Then, when all the nobles came, she pointed to Sir Gawaine.

"He has shown himself the strongest knight we have ever known," said she. "Tell me – for it is for you to decide – shall he guard the waters of the fairy fountain for me, and for all of you?"

The nobles, who knew that Sir Gawaine had conquered in a fair fight, said that he should. And then the lady stood up on her raised throne, walked down the steps, and gave Sir Gawaine her hand.

"Be it so!" said she.

CHAPTER FOURTEEN

SIR TRISTRAM'S ADVENTURE

Sir Tristram was born in a country called Lyonnesse, and his mother was a great Queen, who died when he was only a few hours old. After some years the King, his father, married again and had more children – handsome little sons and pretty little daughters. But their mother, Tristram's stepmother, was very jealous of the Prince, who was the child of her husband's first wife, and she tried to poison him. When the King found out, he was very angry and ordered the wicked stepmother to be burnt. But little Tristram burst into tears when he was told of this terrible punishment. He ran to the King, his father and, kneeling at his feet, begged that his stepmother's life should be spared. So the King pardoned her, and, after he had saved her life, the stepmother simply worshipped the ground upon which the young Prince trod.

He was brought up chiefly in Brittany, and then, when he had grown into a young man, he went to the court of King Mark of Cornwall. There, everybody like him and admired him heartily for his courage and his goodness of heart. He was a musician as well as a knight, and he played the harp as beautifully as any minstrel, so that all the ladies of the court would sit together and whisper about him. They wished he would fall in love with one of them, but, although he was the very soul of courtesy and chivalry, he had no desire to marry.

After a time, he went, as did all young knights in those days, to King Arthur's court and became a knight of the Round Table, while he was still quite young. He fought in many tournaments, and the ladies who watched would say to each other: "Here comes Sir Tristram. See the lions upon his shield!" For the lions were Sir Tristram's coat-of-arms.

Then came a day in Sir Tristram's life which was very wonderful, and yet, in the end, very sad. He was sent to Ireland by King Mark, to bring back a beautiful Princess, called Iseult, who was to be King Mark's bride and take her place as Queen of Cornwall. Sir Tristram set off in a beautiful ship, with shining sails and cabins fitted up in silver and gold. He took his harp with him, and also his shield, his spear, his helmet, and his sword. He did not know whether there might be adventures waiting for him in Ireland.

Sure enough, no sooner had he reached Ireland than he found the King, Princess Iseult's father, in great need of help from the attacks of many enemies. So Sir Tristram put his sword and spear at the King's service and helped him in many a fight, until the Princess Iseult began to think that the young knight who had come to fetch her to Cornwall was the finest knight in the world. So that, when at last they set sail together for Cornwall, after the King of Ireland had conquered his enemies, the two young people were more than half in love with each other.

But Princess Iseult would have married King Mark and probably forgotten Tristram, if it had not been for something that happened on the voyage. You must know that Iseult had taken her lady-in-waiting with her, and that the Queen of Ireland had given this lady a magic drink, in a crystal bottle with a gold stopper. It was a love-drink, a fairy wine, which would make those who drank it together love each other for ever and ever. This love-drink, said the Queen, was to be drunk only by Iseult and King Mark on their wedding-day.

Well, the weather was hot, and the sparkling sea seemed to make it hotter, and Sir Tristram sat on the deck of the fine ship in the sunshine and played his harp to beautiful Iseult. When he laid it down, she asked him to go into the cabin below and bring her something to drink, for she was very thirsty.

Sir Tristram went down, and there, on the table, he saw a pretty crystal bottle with a gold stopper, filled with what looked like sparkling wine. He carried it on deck to Princess Iseult, who took it eagerly into her hand, drew out the gold stopper, and tasted the fragrant drink. It gave her a delicious cool feeling, and she passed the crystal bottle to Sir Tristram and bade him also drink some. He did so – and then they looked at each other in amazement and rapture. They had drunk the fairy drink together, the drink intended for Iseult and King Mark.

Sir Tristram did not speak, but he took up his harp, and he played and sang the most beautiful and yet the saddest lovesong that was ever composed. Iseult sat with her lovely face hidden in her white hands, her dark hair shining like polished ebony in the sunlight. The breeze rustled mournfully in the sails of the ship, and the waves had a sorrowful sound in them, as if the very mermaids and water nymphs were weeping for poor young Sir Tristram and sweet Princess Iseult. For never, never had two lovers felt love like that which had been hidden in the fairy drink, and which could not end in a happy marriage, because Iseult was the promised bride of King Mark.

So Tristram took his dear Princess to Cornwall, and she was married with royal rejoicings, and her sorrowful knight went away and had many great and fine adventure for her sake. But they could never forget what they had felt when they drank the fairy drink, and they were always faithful to each other's memory.

Chapter Eleven: The Fairy Hunt

Arthur and Guinevere were married with
great rejoicings and celebration. Minstrels
with harps played and sang to the King
and Queen.

Chapter Twelve: King Pellinore's Adventure

There, in front of King Pellinore, stood a
great beast, who seemed to have swallowed
up the fairy hounds, for Pellinore
could hear them baying still, from deep inside
the monster.

CHAPTER FIFTEEN

THE PIG-STY PRINCE AND THE MANY TRAVELS

ne of King Arthur's cousins was a little Prince who had been found in a pig-sty. The swineherd who found him, however, knew that he was a Prince and took him up to the King's palace, where, after a little time, the King acknowledged him as heir to the kingdom. The Prince's own mother was dead, but his stepmother, who was very fond of him, was determined that he should marry well. When he was grown up, therefore, she told him that only one Princess in the world was worthy of him, and that was the Princess Olwen.

The Pig-Sty Prince (everybody knew him by this name) immediately determined to marry the Princess Olwen and set off to King Arthur's court to ask him for her hand as a kingly gift. For, in those days, anybody who wanted anything hurried off to ask King Arthur to give it to him. When the Prince reached King Arthur's palace, the doorkeeper thought he had never seen so fine a man and admitted him immediately. The Pig-Sty Prince begged the

King to give him the hand of the Princess Olwen, and the King said he would gladly have consented had he ever heard of her. As he had not, he sent out messengers who spent twelve months in looking for her, but were no wiser on the last day of the year than they had been on the first.

But King Arthur was too great a King to permit even a Pig-Sty Prince to go home disappointed and empty-handed. He summoned the bravest and strongest of his knights and warriors, and bade them set off with the Prince in search of the Princess Olwen. So this wonderful band of strong and brave men rode away into the country; and, after some weeks of travel they saw a great castle in the distance. Just as they arrived within calling distance of it, they came upon an immense flock of sheep in charge of a shepherd; so they rode up to him and asked him to whom the castle belonged. He answered that it belonged to the father of the Princess Olwen.

Then these warriors from Arthur's court said that they had come to take the Princess Olwen to the King. Whereupon the shepherd told them that other strong and brave men had gone into the castle on the same quest, but that none had come out alive. He told them, too, that he was the brother of the lord of the castle, who had stolen all his possessions from him and made him shepherd of the castle sheep. Then, the Pig-Sty Prince gave him a ring, which the shepherd took home and showed to his wife, who was very much pleased and excited, for the ring was a family treasure, and she knew, by what her husband told her, that her own sister's son was near at hand. As she was talking to the shepherd about the ring, all King Arthur's messengers rode up to the house, with the Pig-Sty Prince in the middle of them. The shepherd's wife greeted them and showed great joy at meeting with her nephew.

Then the shepherd's wife told her visitors that sometimes the Princess Olwen came to the cottage to wash her beautiful auburn hair, and that, if a message was sent to her, she might come that very night. So a message was sent, and, sure enough, the Princess came.

The moment that the Pig-Sty Prince saw her, he recognized her, and he fell even more deeply in love with her real self than he had been with the image of her in his fancy. She, too, fell in love with him, but told him she was afraid he could never win her. His only chance, she said, was to ask her father for her hand and to promise to perform every task which the cruel lord should command. Then she mounted her beautiful white pony and went back to the castle.

The lord of the castle was a terrible-looking man, almost hidden in his own wild long hair. Three times he tried to drive Arthur's messengers away with poisoned arrows, but, each time, they caught the

arrows and flung them back at the lord. So at last –
as he was very badly hurt by the arrows – he bade
them declare their desire.

Then Arthur's warriors put the Pig-Sty Prince in a
chair opposite the great chair in which the cruel lord
sat. And the two began to argue, one against the
other.

"You must root up the whole of that hill yonder,"
said the father of Princess Olwen; "you must till it
and sow it in one day, and in one day the wheat must
grow and ripen. Of that wheat, only, shall bread be
baked for my daughter's wedding."

"It will be quite easy for me to do this," answered
the Pig-Sty Prince, remembering what Olwen had
told him about promising to do all that he was asked.

"This may be easy, but there are other things
which you cannot do. Only two men in the world can
till the land and rid it of its stones. Neither of them
will work for you, and you will not be able to make
them. Another man has in his possession the only
oxen that can possibly pull a tiller over such wild
country. He will not give them up to you, and you
will not be able to get them. When first I met
Olwen's mother, nine bushels of flax were sown, and,
from the seed, not a blade came up. I require you to
recover the flax and to sow it again in the wild land
worked by the men who will not come, and tilled by
the oxen you cannot get. When the flax has grown, it

must make the linen for the head-dress my daughter is to wear at her wedding."

"It will be perfectly easy for me to do all these things," cried the Pig-Sty Prince valiantly.

"You may be able to sow the flax and reap it," said the lord of the castle, "but there are other things you certainly cannot do. I want honey that is nine times sweeter than comb-honey, to put into the marriage drink, and I must have the famous cup of which so many stories are told, to hold this sweet drink of wine. Also, you must bring me the fairy horn, and the fairy harp, and the fairy cauldron of which all the world has heard tell. Then I must certainly wash my head and shave my beard for the ceremony, and I can only shave with the great boar's razor. Nor can I spread out my hair in order to wash it unless I have blood from the jet-black witch."

"All these things I can easily get for you," boasted the Pig-Sty Prince.

"Yes, but, even if I wash my head, my hair is so thick and matted I can comb it only with the fairy comb and cut off its ends with the fairy scissors, that hang between the two ears of the great enchanted boar who also carries the razor."

"It will be perfectly easy for me to hunt the great enchanted boar and bring you the comb and scissors as well as the razor," shouted the Pig-Sty Prince at the top of his voice.

"In order to do so, you will want the fairy hound, and the fairy leash to hold him, and the fairy collar and chain, and the great huntsman whose name is Mabon, who was stolen from his mother when he was three days old and has been lost ever since. Whatever else you can do, you cannot find Mabon."

"It will be the easiest thing in the world for me to find Mabon. What else is there for me to do?" demanded the persistent lover of the Princess Olwen.

It appeared that there were various other things for him to do, one of which was to persuade King Arthur to join in the hunt for the enchanted boar with the razor. The lord of the castle was quite sure that King Arthur would refuse to do any such thing – but the Pig-Sty Prince knew better. Last of all his tasks was to bring Olwen's father the sword of a terrible giant. This giant could only be slain by his own sword and would certainly kill anyone who tried to steal it from him. But the Pig-Sty Prince was not daunted.

"My lord and kinsman, King Arthur, will obtain all these marvels for me!" he cried fearlessly. "I will have not only your daughter, O great lord with the unkempt hair, but I will have also your life!"

So saying, he departed from the castle, and all King Arthur's warriors departed with him.

They journeyed for a whole day and, in the evening, arrived at another castle, where a giant, who was as black as ebony met them at the gate. When they asked him whose castle it was, he said that it belonged to the giant with the mighty sword, and nobody who went into it ever came out alive. In spite of that, Arthur's warriors went on and knocked at the door. The porter who sat inside called out to them that nobody could be admitted unless he could do something nobody else could do so well. Whereupon Sir Kay, who was among the warriors, answered that he was the finest polisher of swords in the world.

The porter carried this news to the giant, who replied that his sword needed polishing very badly, and ordered that Sir Kay should be admitted. So Sir Kay was let into the castle, and the sword was given into his hand; and, after polishing it and making it very sharp, he slipped behind the giant and cut off his head!

Then all the warriors rushed into the giant's castle and took the gold and silver that were hidden in it. With this treasure, and with the great sword, they went back to Arthur's court and told him the whole story. And, when Arthur heard of the other marvels that had yet to be performed, he asked which of them had better be undertaken first. In answer, the warriors told him that it would be best to find Mabon, the lost huntsman, who was stolen from his mother when he was three days old.

Now, of course, Mabon had been stolen by the

fairy-people, and only the fairy-people would be able to tell of his hiding-place. Very close to the fairy-people lived the birds in the trees. So, first of all, the warriors went in search of the talking blackbird.

They found the blackbird flying about a glen, and, when they asked her where Mabon could be found, she said she would show them the way to a certain fairy stag, who might be able to help them, as he was many years older than she was. So off they all set to find the fairy stag. When they found him, they told him that they were the messengers of King Arthur, and that they were seeking Mabon.

The stag answered that there was an owl who was much older than he was, and who might possibly be able to answer their question. As they were Arthur's messengers, he added, he would lead them to the owl. Once more, they formed a procession, with the stag and the blackbird in front, and moved on over the hills till they found the fairy owl.

But the owl could not tell them where Mabon had been hidden. All he could do was to lead them to another bird, still older than himelf – the great eagle of the crags. And the eagle it was who told them of the great and wonderful fairy salmon.

The eagle had once tried to kill the salmon, but they had become friends afterwards, and so, when the mighty bird led Arthur's messengers to the mighty fish, the salmon answered that he knew where

Mabon was, and he took two of the messengers upon his wide silver sholders and swam up the river with them to the stone walls of an old city. And there they heard someone crying and lamenting in a dungeon – and it was Mabon, who had been stolen from his mother when he was only three days old.

Then the warriors went back to Arthur's court, and the King gathered together an army and came to the old stone city and attacked the dungeon and set Mabon free and took him home. And then they all began to ask each other which marvel it would be best that they should next seek.

The fairy hound and the fairy leash and the fairy collar had still to be discovered. As Sir Kay was talking all this over with Sir Bedivere, they suddenly saw a great smoke from a great fire, and they thought it was the fire of a robber. They hurried off in the direction of the fire, and there, sure enough, was the greatest robber that Arthur had ever hunted, roasting some boar's flesh on a spit. And Sir Kay, pointing to the robber's beard, whispered to Sir Bedivere that only the living hairs from that beard could make the fairy leash that would hold the fairy hound with which Mabon must hunt the enchanted boar who carried the comb and the scissors and the razor.

So the two warriors hid themselves until the robber had eaten so much supper that he fell fast asleep. Then they stole up to him and actually managed, not only to dig a great pit under his feet while he slept, but to tip him into it without waking him up. When he was fast in the pit, they plucked out the hair of his beard, and then killed him, as he was a very wicked robber.

Carrying the leash which they had made of the robber's beard, they returned to Arthur's court. "Now," said King Arthur, "what is to be the next marvel?" And they all agreed that it was to be the capture of the fairy hound.

They had to search through many countries, but at last they found the fairy hound in the Enchanted Forest itself and took it home to Arthur's castle. And now they were all ready to hunt the boar. But it was such a great and terrible animal that Arthur said they would not start upon the hunt until they were quite sure it really *had* the comb and scissors hanging between its ears. So he made one of his knights take the form of a bird and fly to the mountain where the enchanted boar was hidden. He flew right down on top of the boar's den, and, sure enough, there were the comb, and the scissors, and the razor.

For a time, Arthur decided to leave the boar alone and obtain the magic cauldron. Now, the cauldron was in the house of a great king, who kept all his money in it and entirely refused to part with it at Arthur's request. So Arthur made war on him and conquered him, and carried away the cauldron.

And now the day had arrived for the great hunting, but all the enchanted boars of the country heard of it, and turned out, themselves, to fight the warriors of Arthur's court. Chief among these great boars was a huge beast with bristles like silver wire, that made a shining pathway as he rushed through the trees. Arthur's warriors and Mabon and the fairy hound had terrible battles with the boars; but at last, the great beast with the comb and the scissors and the razor was driven into the river, not far from the very city where Mabon had been found by the two knights who rode on the shoulders of the fairy salmon.

Then, while the huge creature lashed the water, Mabon himself sprang upon it and snatched the razor from its tusk and hid it under his vest. But nobody could reach the comb and the scissors, until a very brave warrior followed Mabon into the water and managed to get hold of the scissors. However, before either man could secure the comb, the boar scrambled out of the water and galloped off. Then King Arthur himself set off after it with a whole host of knights. At last they overtook it, and, after a ter-rific fight, got possession of the comb. Then, the enchanted boar was driven into the ocean and never seen again.

Then King Arthur and his warriors took a short rest, after which the King asked if there were still any more marvels to be performed. And his knights answered that the blood of the black witch had yet to be obtained. So the king set off in search of the black witch and found her hiding in a cave, and she nearly killed two of the warriors the moment they entered her hiding-place. So King Arthur instantly took his sword and leapt into the cave and cut the ugly black witch in two. And one of his attendants took the fairy blood and put it into a fairy basin.

Now, as Arthur's messengers had got the witch's blood and the magical razor and the fairy comb and scissors, they thought that the other tasks might wait awhile, and they all went to the horrible lord's castle with their spoils. They sprinkled his hair and beard with the witch's blood, and then, in spite of his struggles, cut both of them off and shaved him as clean as an ivory ball. Then, as the loss of his hair and beard made him quite helpless, they found it easy to chop off his head with the giant's sword. After that, they took possession of the castle and all the gold and silver and jewels that were hidden in it.

As the father of the Princess was dead, there was really no need now to trouble about the other marvels that he had declared were to be performed for her wedding day. The Pig-Sty Prince therefore married her without them, and he and his bride and Arthur's knights and warriors feasted for at least a week in the castle.

CHAPTER SIXTEEN

THE KNIGHT OF THE SPARROW-HAWK

ing Arthur held his court not only at beautiful Camelot, but also at a place called Caerlon. The castle there had seven doors, with a magnificent porter seated at each one, to open and shut it when the knights and ladies passed.

Well, one evening, a handsome unknown youth, dressed in yellow satin, came running up to the castle and told a porter that there was a mysterious white stag in the woods over the river. The porter hurried to tell Arthur; for, ever since the Fairy Hunt of which you have read, the King had vowed there should never be a white stag near his castle that he would not follow. So, as soon as the dawn broke next morning, the whole court set off a-hunting – horns blowing, hounds baying, and horses prancing. The white stag meant a fairy adventure for one of the knights, of that everybody was certain.

Now, Queen Guinevere was late that morning, and the hunt was almost out of sight when she came tripping down the stone stairs into the castle hall. She asked where Arthur had gone and was told by her ladies that he had ridden off to hunt a great white stag in the ferny woods. Guinevere pouted for a minute; then, all at once, she clapped her hands joyfully and declared that she would go a-hunting after the King! So she and her maidens dressed themselves quickly and set off on horseback.

As they rode through the trees, they heard a great galloping behind them, and up came one of the very handsomest knights of the Round Table. He had long golden hair, and a long golden sword, and a blue-purple scarf, with a golden apple at every corner round his shoulders. His legs were bare, the better to grip the sides of his horse, which was very strong and tall and had a long black mane and a tail that was even blacker and longer.

"It is good young Geraint!" cried the ladies. "Oh, handsome and brave Geraint, are you coming with us and with the Queen?"

Now, Geraint had really intended to gallop after Arthur as fast as he could, for he, too, was late this morning. But, when the ladies asked him if he were going to escort the Queen, he could not possibly say he was not. So he bowed very low, drew in his prancing horse, and joined the pretty company of maidens, giving up all idea of an adventure.

But, no sooner had he drawn near the side of the Queen, than the adventure, which he thought he had given up, came riding through the woods towards him, in the shape of an enormous knight with his face

Chapter Twelve: King Pellinore's Adventure

The black knight rushed at King Pellinore, and they fought until the forest rang with noise. The King won the fight easily and fairly, and he and the beautiful fairy-lady returned to Camelot.

Chapter Thirteen: Sir Gawaine's Adventure

The beautiful fairy-maiden took Sir Gawaine's shield and rubbed it bright and clean for him.

quite hidden under his helmet. On one side of this giant stranger rode a lady dressed in rich brocade, on the other pranced a hideous little dwarf. As they trotted abreast through the wood, Guinevere pulled up her horse and stared at them in amazement. Then the newcomers also drew rein, and, standing still at a little distance, seemed to talk among themselves.

The Queen, frankly curious, shook her horse's bridle and trotted off across the turf to speak to them. The dwarf was the nearest to her, and, pausing as she came up to him, she asked him the name of the big knight with the hidden face. But the dwarf, who was the ugliest little man you ever saw in your life, answered by striking the Queen with a long wand that he carried in his hand.

Then, such a shout as you never heard before rang through the woods from Geraint! All the ladies, too, cried out in anger. Before anybody could do anything, however, off galloped the strange knight, with the lady and the dwarf on either hand. And off after them tore young Geraint, calling that he would avenge the Queen!

Such a chase the three led him, right through the woods, and over the mountain, and down into a valley where you could see the towers and roofs of a great city. Through the gates they rode, with Geraint still hard on their heels. He saw that all the people stood still and saluted the knight and the lady as they galloped past; and he noticed, even in his haste, that the courtyards of the houses were full of men, who were polishing shields, and burnishing swords, and washing armour, and shoeing horses. Then the knight and the dwarf and the lady galloped up a hill to a great castle. Its gates were immediately opened with sounds of welcome. The three rode in, and the entrance was closed and barred behind them.

As Geraint pulled up his horse, weary and bitterly disappointed, he saw that he was close to a ruined palace, which could be approached by way of an old marble bridge that spanned a deep river. He crossed the bridge and was met on the other side by an old man, who wore very ragged clothing, but whose voice was gentle and manner gracious. This old man invited the knight into the ruined palace, where he was met by an old woman, also in rags, but sweet and dignified. With her was her daughter, whose face and hair were beautiful above her poor rough clothing. They, too, greeted Geraint in soft voices and offered him meat and drink.

As he ate, the beautiful girl, who was named Enid, looked after his horse, and he watched her with deep admiration in his eyes. Then the poor old couple told him that they were the real lord and lady of the city, but had been turned out of their home by the Knight of the Sparrow-Hawk. He was the knight whom Geraint had been following, and he lived now in the castle, and every year he held a tournament in the meadow just below it. In this meadow, a Sparrow-Hawk, set up between two high three-pronged spears, was always the prize of the day. Whoever won it was called "Knight of the Sparrow-Hawk" for a whole year, with the right to live in the castle and to rule over the land. But, as the knight himself always won, by fair means or foul, there was not really much use in anybody else doing battle for the prize.

Geraint listened, and his heart beat high with hope. "*I* will fight for the Sparrow-Hawk tomorrow," he cried. "I will conquer the knight whose dwarf insulted Queen Guinevere, and I will force him to return your castle and your riches to you, from whom he stole them."

The poor old couple shook their heads.

"No knight can fight for the Sparrow-Hawk unless the lady is with him whom he thinks the fairest lady in the world. Long ago, this magic was made in the meadow. It is because the Knight of the Sparrow-Hawk never stirs without his lady that he is always able to win."

"His lady may be beautiful, but she is not half so beautiful as your daughter yonder!" cried Geraint eagerly.

The words were no sooner out of his mouth than the old couple rose to their feet in great excitement.

"If you indeed believe that," said they, "take our

daughter with you into the meadow tomorrow! We will find arms for you, and she will make it possible for you to win."

The next morning dawned beautiful and clear, and a great gathering came together, very early indeed, in the meadow where the Sparrow-Hawk was set up between the two three-pronged spears. When everybody had arrived, a great blast of trumpets was blown at the castle gates. They were flung open, and out rode the enormous knight, with, as usual, the dwarf upon his right hand, and the lady upon his left. He drew rein, and his heralds cried out the proclamation. Was there anyone present who would come forward and fight for the Sparrow-Hawk?

Nobody stirred, and the great knight turned to his lady and bade her go, take the Sparrow-Hawk upon her hand, and bring it to him. But, just as she was about to set off, a young knight in old rusty armour, on a very tired, half-lame horse, rode forward; at his side, a maiden in rags walked quietly, with neither shoes nor stockings upon her little white feet, and only a coarse hood upon her head.

"My lady is fairer than yours!" shouted young Geraint. "Come! I will fight you for the Sparrow-Hawk and call down the magic of the meadow to help me!"

Then the two knights rushed upon each other with a great crash of arms, while the lady in the rich brocade and the lady in rags looked on. Everybody had burst out laughing at Geraint and his rusty battledress. But soon their laughter changed to amazement and admiration, for, with right goodwill, the young stranger hacked and struck, until he proved himself by far the cleverer and stronger. And at last, a great ringing shout went up from the whole multitude of watchers, for they saw the great knight of the castle thrown to the ground, stunned and motionless, while Geraint rode up to the Sparrow-Hawk, took it upon his wrist, and, carrying it to a very old man and a very old woman among the crowd, presented it to them with the grace of a prince making an offering to his lawful king and queen.

Then another shout went up from the people! They recognized in the poor beggars their rightful lady and their rightful lord. Leaving Geraint to look after the fallen knight, they escorted the old man and woman back into the castle that had been stolen from them. There Geraint presently followed, with beautiful Enid, and with the great defeated knight bound in chains. As for the lady and the dwarf, they had already fled. But all the people were shouting with excitement and gladness; for, indeed, they were delighted to see their true lord and lady restored to their own home.

Then sweet Enid went upstairs to her own dainty chamber and dressed herself in soft silks and a gossamer veil. She came down, looking like a princess, and Geraint fell more deeply in love with her than ever. He said he would take her to Arthur's court, and there they would be married. Also, he explained, he could not marry his fair lady until the insult to Queen Guinevere had been wiped out.

So they set off: Geraint and his lady, and the knight in chains behind.

When they reached Caerlon, Geraint led both his bride and his prisoner into the presence of the Queen. The big knight apologized as humble as anyone could wish and was sent away again. Geraint married Enid, with everyone's full approval, and the Queen herself gave the wedding dress, and the happy pair remined at the court of King Arthur for the rest of their lives.

CHAPTER SEVENTEEN

THE LITTLE PRINCE OF THE LAKE

fter the day when King Arthur and King Pellinore and Sir Gawaine had followed the elfin hunt into the heart of Fairyland, most wonderful adventures began to happen, not only to them, but to all the other knights of the Round Table. To brave the mysterious dangers of the Enchanted Forest, and the Castle Perilous, and the Valley of No Return, was the greatest sign of courage that anyone could show. So, of course, when the King came back again and told of the things that he had seen and heard, every one of his followers wanted to go into Fairyland and see these marvels for themselves. One by one they went; and, on their return, they told the story of their adventures. The fame of Arthur's fearless knights was soon spread far and wide. Every brave and romantic youth wanted to come and make his vow of fealty to the great King who was the head of such a gallant company. And among these youths was a Prince called Lancelot, who had spent all his childhood in Fairyland, in a way that you shall read about.

He was the son of a great King named Ban, whose

castle was built in a valley between two mountain ranges. When Lancelot was only a little baby, a nearby King, called Claudas, came riding one day over the eastern range with an enormous army behind him. This great, glittering army set up its tents all around King Ban's castle and prepared to besiege it. For a long time, King Ban and his soldiers held out against King Claudas and the big army; but, at last, they had to give in.

So then King Ban sent a messenger to King Claudas, asking leave for himself, and the Queen and their little son, to leave their home and to go and place themselves under the protection of the great King Arthur. Claudas consented, but only on condition that the castle was handed over to him immediately. So poor King Ban handed over his castle and set off very, very sorrowfully, on a big horse, with the weeping Queen in the saddle behind him. On a second horse rode just one faithful servant, carrying the baby prince, Lancelot.

They rode a little way down the valley, and then King Ban said he could not bear to leave his beautiful castle without one look at it from the top of the nearest hill. So the Queen took the baby into her arms and sat down by the side of a beautiful clear lake; while the King and the faithful servant rode together to the top of the mountain.

For a long time after the sound of their horses' feet

had passed away, everything was very quiet in the valley. The Queen, who had dried her tears, played almost contentedly with the baby, consoled by its beauty and its merriment. By and by, however, she became anxious, for she thought that the King had been away a very long time. The baby was asleep by now, so she laid it down among the meadow flowers, covered it with her cloak, and set off, on foot, up the rocky path that led to the top of the hill.

She had not gone more than a hundred yards or so when she heard a queer chuckling laugh behind her – just like the chuckle of a water hen among the rushes, only much longer and more mischievous. She turned around quickly. And what do you think she saw?

She saw her little baby, the most precious thing she had, in the arms of a strange and beautiful lady. This lady's gown rippled about her like water in the moonlight; her long golden hair was wreathed with forget-me-nots and silver shells; her white arms shone like alabaster. She had taken the baby to a big black rock that jutted out from the land towards the middle of the lake. She was rocking it in her arms and laughing. At the moment the Queen caught sight of her, she began to sing.

The words seemed to be a fairy lullaby, but the poor Queen did not pause to listen. With a loud cry, she set off running, to rescue her little baby. But the fairy saw her coming. She sprang up on the rock, joined her two pretty white feet together, and, with the baby still in her arms, dived, like a silver shining arrow, straight into the green waters of the lake. A sound like a clap of thunder echoed all down the valley, and a sudden wind lashed the water into white foam. The lightning played among the trees, like the flames of a witch's fire; and long, loud peals of laughter mingled with the terrible storm. It lasted just for a minute, then went as suddenly as it had come. Everything was still again; the lake glimmered green and calm. But the fairy and the baby had disappeared.

The poor distracted Queen ran up and down the banks of the lake, wringing her hands and calling out her baby's name. As she wept and called, the faithful servant came hurrying down the side of the mountain. He, too, was sobbing. He said that wicked King Claudas had set fire to the castle, which was blazing away into ruins; and that King Ban was lying at the top of the hill, dead with grief.

Then the Queen dried her eyes, and folded her hands, and spoke calmly:

"My husband has gone. My baby has gone. My home has gone," she said. "There is nothing left for me to live for. I may as well die, too."

But, even as she said this, the Abbess of a convent not far away, came walking, wrapped in her cloak, along the banks of the lake. She was a good and sweet woman, and she knew all about the fairy in the silver robes, with white hands and golden hair, who lived under the water. She heard the Queen's sad words, and, coming up to her, she spoke consolingly.

"Poor Queen!" she said – "for, indeed, I know you are a Queen – be comforted! You have not lost as much as you think you have. Your little baby is in hands far safer than those of any human nurse! For your husband, the King, be content. He is at peace. For yourself, there is a home waiting in the convent among the trees. Dry your tears and come with me."

The Abbess spoke so gently, and yet so firmly, that somehow an extraordinary feeling of consolation came over the poor Queen. She went to the convent with this good woman and found it was a beautiful and restful place. The Abbess kept telling her that the baby was, indeed, in the very best of hands. So by and by, the Queen, who was tired of wars and troubles, settled down in contentment and stayed with the good Abbess in the convent until she died.

But what had happened to the baby?

Well, the beautiful fairy dived down, down, down, carrying little Lancelot in her arms. As she dived, her silver gown mingled with the silver ripples. Then, far below her, appeared the roofs and towers of an enchanted city. And now the water turned into a cloudy mist, and her robes spread out into two glittering wings. She was no longer diving, but floating on the misty air. Softly, very softly, she floated downwards, till the bright streets, and flowery gardens, and marble walls of the enchanted city showed quite clearly beneath. Then she stretched out her little white feet, and alighted on the very tips of her toes, among the tall green grass and all the fairy butter-cups and daisies. And from every side, beautiful ladies came running up to her, exclaiming, and shouting, and clapping their hands. They were, every one of them, fairies of the lake, and they were so pleased to have got a little human baby that they did not know what to do.

Tiny Lancelot had been sleeping all this time, and, because he was in the arms of a water-fairy, had been able to breathe quite comfortably all the way down through the lake. Now he woke up and smiled at the pretty ladies clustering around him. Then they took him into one of the enchanted houses and gave him a wonderful nursery all to himself. And he was so merry and healthy that they called him the "beautiful foundling." But the fairy-lady who had brought him there, and who was the Queen of them all, called him "Son of a King." Because, you see, she knew that he was of royal human blood, and that, some day, he must go back to the world, from Fairyland, and play his part, as a Prince, among his fellow-men.

And how Lancelot of the Lake went back to the world from the enchanted city under the water, you shall hear in another story.

CHAPTER EIGHTEEN
THE WIZARD BEWITCHED

Merlin was growing very old now, and his work at Arthur's court was nearly finished. He had made the Round Table for the knights who took the great Vow; and he had set the Seat Perilous at the King's right hand. No knight had ventured to take his place on that mysterious seat yet. If ever one, or another, approached it, the fiery letters would suddenly shine out, in golden flame: "This is the Seat Perilous."

The great magician let his beard grow very long and white, and he would sit outside the great doors of Camelot, singing to himself, and playing on a harp that he held in his long magician's fingers. And with him, very often, in those days, would sit the fairy Nimue, who was one of the Ladies of the Lake.

She had changed her name to Vivian; Nimue was too strange a title for any human lady to bear. Since King Pellinore had brought her back to Arthur's court, she had behaved as much like a flesh-and-blood princess as she could. But she was never anything, really, but one of the Ladies of the Lake — a mysterious elfin thing, with mermaid's eyes that were green and dark. She knew a lot of magic herself, and, in the old days, she had often peeped in at Merlin, as he sat in his house with the seventy windows and the sixty doors. It had been in obedience to the old wizard's orders that she had helped to make the wonderful and high adventure of the Fairy Hunt, which had carried King Arthur into the Enchanted Forest so soon after his wedding day. And now, it seemed to her, the old magician was growing weary of the world; and she thought that it would be nice for him to go away and live forever in Fairyland.

Often she would persuade him to sing to her and, also, to tell her stories of the magic that he had made in his life. Her eyes would grow dark and bright with excitement as she listened, and she would twist her golden hair around her white fingers and tap her little feet on the grass. Then she would ask him to walk with her in the woods and meadows, and she would make wreaths of wild roses and lilies and hang them on her pretty neck and arms, as they talked.

Then she would try to make him speak of the Silver Table, and the Rich Fisher, and the Shining Cup; and ask him where he had hidden the little book in which it was all written down. But this Merlin would never tell her. For he knew well enough that she was only a fairy from Fairyland. Yet she fascinated him more and more! Because, you see, he kept telling her secret after secret, so that she was spinning webs of

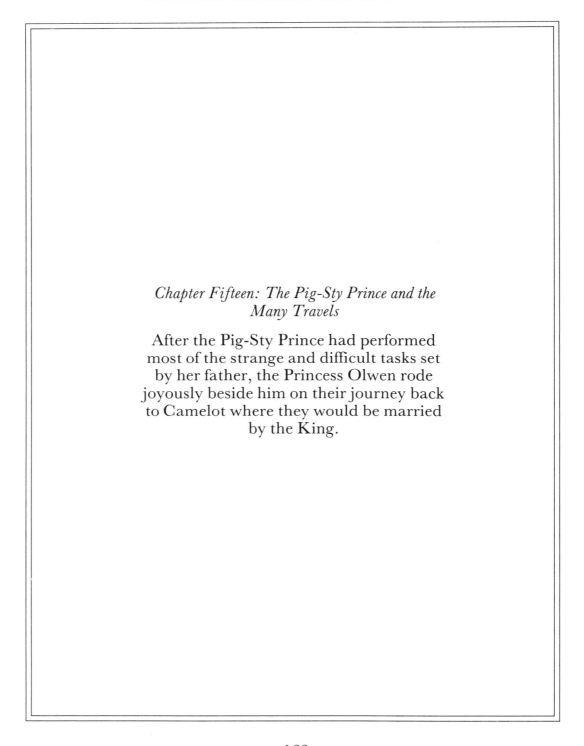

*Chapter Fifteen: The Pig-Sty Prince and the
Many Travels*

After the Pig-Sty Prince had performed
most of the strange and difficult tasks set
by her father, the Princess Olwen rode
joyously beside him on their journey back
to Camelot where they would be married
by the King.

Chapter Eighteen: The Wizard Bewitched

The beautiful Vivian, the Lady of the Lake, pleaded with Merlin to go with her to the mysterious fountain of Broceliande, where he would be able to sleep forever in the peace of the fairy mist.

his own magic about him all the time.

One night, they had been wandering in the woods together, and Merlin, cold and weary, was walking slowly home, alone. Vivian still lingered by the side of a lake in which were bright reflections of the stars. Tonight, he was thinking deeply of Arthur and all the other knights of the Round Table. Above all, he was wondering when that knight would come who could sit safely in the Seat Perilous. Because Merlin knew that this knight, and only he, would be the knight who would be able to go into that far mysterious place where Joseph had hidden the Silver Table and the Holy Grail.

As he thought about these things, all at once a voice came through the trees, and he saw an old, old man leaning upon his staff, who spoke his name, "Merlin."

"Who are you?" said Merlin, startled.

"I am Blaise, the hermit who christened you many, many years ago. Merlin, I have come to warn you. Your own enchantments are being woven around you! If you go on teaching your Lady of the Lake any more secrets, she will cast a spell on you that even you will not be able to break."

Merlin sighed. "Good Blaise," said he, "what am I but half a fairy, myself! I have done, I think, all that I was meant to do. I have set King Arthur on the throne of his father; I have made the Round Table; I

have explained the letters written in the Seat Perilous. The Shining Cup is still hidden, but I do not
think I am meant to wait at Arthur's court until it is
found. I would be glad to go into some far country –
say, to Broceliande – and to rest there in the green
forests for ever."

Blaise waited a minute or two, then spoke again.

"It may be as you say," he answered. "Perhaps
your work is really done. It has been a good work,
Merlin. The wicked mountain demons have lost
much of their power since the Round Table was
made. They will lose it all when once the Shining
Cup has been found again. So go your way, Merlin!
Rest if you like, forever, by the side of the woodland
fountain, under the branches of the tall green tree!"

The hermit's voice died away; and, even while
Merlin looked, Blaise seemed to be swallowed up in
the shadows of the woods. But, slipping starrily
through the trees, he saw the bright nymph, Vivian,
coming to him again.

"Great wizard," she said, putting her little cool
hand in his. "Come! Come away with me to Brittany!
Come to Broceliande!"

Merlin laid his arm around her shoulders. "If I
should go with you to Broceliande," he said, "I do
not think that I should ever come back!"

"Never mind," whispered the fairy. "Only come!"

She drew him across the dim dewy meadows until

they reached the sea. There, under the stars, a little boat was rocking – one of the fairy boats that belonged to the Ladies of the Lake.

"Come!" whispered Vivian once more. And this time Merlin gave way without another word.

So they sailed away to Brittany, and to Broceliande, where the green tree grew over the magical fountain that Gawaine, and only Gawaine, had found. But the Lady of the Lake knew every inch of the ferny path that led to it.

Then, before them, they saw whitethorn bushes glimmering pale, and, above the bushes, the tall green tree. They reached the fairy fountain and sat down beside it.

"See!" said Vivian. "Here is the white marble slab, and the silver bowl fastened with the silver chain! But no knight is guarding the fairy well tonight!"

"Why should it be guarded?" asked Merlin, laying his hand on the marble. "The fountain is mine – has always been mine! The secrets of its waters are mine. This white stone is mine. See! My name is written there!"

Vivian looked, and sure enough, she saw letters of gold appear, just for a moment, on the marble slab:

"I am the Stone of Merlin."

They shone there, exactly like the letters on the Seat

Perilous, and then they faded away. The fairy drew nearer to the wizard, and he laid one hand on her hair; while, with the other, he fingered the silver bowl.

"Are all the secrets of Fairyland yours, Merlin?"

"Most of them, sweet Lady of the Lake. Most of them! They are strange secrets, but the greatest of all lies under the stone!"

"What is it? Tell me! What is it?"

"It is the secret of Sleep," said Merlin dreamily. "Of Sleep that can make a man lie and dream from day to day, from month to month, from year to year. I could almost wish I were folded in such a strange sweet Sleep."

"Tell me!" said the fairy again. "Tell me!"

And so Merlin told her, at last, the song and the dance that would draw from that mysterious stone its great secret of unending Sleep.

Then the fairy stood up, and, while he watched her, still dreamily, she began to sing, very softly, and to weave a fairy ring all around the tired old wizard, and the white marble slab, and the magic pool. And, as she sang and danced, Merlin's weary eyes closed, and his head drooped low on his chest, down which streamed his white long beard. Then a little silver mist, like pearly air, crept up from the fountain, and out from underneath the fairy stone. And the magician's head bent lower and lower, until, at last, he lay beside the mysterious fountain in Broceliande, fast asleep.

Vivian stopped singing and dancing, and stood looking at him in the moonlight, her eyes more like green water than ever. The leaf shadows flickered over her and over the sleeping wizard, and the pearly mist grew thicker. And gathering her gleaming robes around her, she slid away like a silver shadow, back to her own enchanted waters, leaving Merlin sleeping soundly and calmly in the fairy mist under the tall green tree.

CHAPTER NINETEEN

THE ADVENTURE OF SIR BORS

ir Bors was a very big knight, tall and strong, as you might have guessed from the sound of his name. One day, he was riding along a grassy road, when he saw a building with high stone walls and towers like a castle, half-hidden among great clumps of fine trees. A river ran around it; and across the river a stone bridge arched.

The look of the castle attracted Sir Bors very much. He turned his horse's head that way and, trotting over the bridge, drew near to the handsome building. A knight rode out through the gates and tried to block his way. But Sir Bors fought with him and conquered him. Then, sparing the other's life, he rode proudly into the courtyard of the castle and was met by the King who owned it.

The King's name was Pelles, and he was always ready to welcome a brave and merciful knight. He greeted Sir Bors courteously and led him into the great hall. And, no sooner was Sir Bors inside, than he felt a strange awe and wonder creeping over him. It seemed to him that this castle was not like any other castle in the world.

It was full of such strange lights and shadows, such whisperings and rustlings, such coolness and perfume. Little birds, like jewels, flew about the gold and purple glass of the windows. Their wings were almost transparent, their heads bore tiny crowns. And, prettiest of all among them, was a white one, like a tiny dove, that flitted through the shadowy hall, carrying in her bill a little golden goblet hung on three chains.

Then, while the dove still flitted about the hall, a table mysteriously appeared, covered with honeyed cakes, and ripe fruits, and crystal goblets filled with crimson wine. The knight and the King sat down to eat and drink. When they had finished, Sir Bors felt so light in body, so refreshed, so calm and rested, that he wondered what sort of fairy food he had been eating. As he wondered he looked up and saw King Pelles watching him.

"Sir Bors," said the King, gently and gravely, "you have always been a good and pure knight."

"I hope so," answered Sir Bors.

"You must have been," replied the King, "or you would never have seen the little white dove and eaten the mysterious food on the mysterious table. And now you will see something still more wonderful.

As the King finished speaking, the hall grew darker, and, at the far end, a golden light appeared. Then, in the heart of the golden light which floated all around her like a sunset cloud, appeared a slim and beautiful lady who, Sir Bors thought, looked like a fair Princess. But, when he looked again, he saw she was not flesh and blood at all. She seemed a sort of delicate spirit, and she moved like a spirit through the dim shadows of the hall. Her feet barely touched the floor. Her hair shone like sunlight, pale wings folded upon her shoulders, and pale hands clasped around what looked like a wondrously beautiful Silver Cup. From the mouth of the cup rose a still flame like the flame of a candle; it was as if this flame shed all the brightness which surrounded the maiden's form.

She passed slowly by, and Sir Bors watched, breathless. Then he turned to King Pelles.

"Who is she?" he asked under his breath. "What is the Cup that she carries?"

The King answered in a mysterious voice.

"She is – who she is! Of the Cup you have heard."

"Is it," whispered Sir Bors, "can it be the Cup of the spirit-world – the silver chalice that we knights call the Holy Grail?"

"Yes," replied King Pelles. "It is the Holy Grail. Here, in this castle, it has been hidden for years. But look again!"

Then Sir Bors looked again, and down the hall, in the very track of the golden maiden, stepping through the lingering fading radiance she had left, came a Princess with a tiny sleeping baby in her arms. She stepped softly towards Sir Bors and held the baby towards him, for him to look at. He thought he had never seen a lady so lovely.

"This is my daughter, the Princess Elaine," said the King, speaking more softly than ever. "And the little child is her son, Galahad. He has been born in the Castle of the Hidden Grail. He it will be who will sit in the Seat Perilous one day, on the right hand of King Arthur, the seat that has been empty so long. But when Galahad takes his seat there –"

"What?" asked Sir Bors, touching the child very gently with his big forefinger. "What?"

But King Pelles did not answer. He shook his head and fell silent again. The Princess Elaine smiled down at her little baby, and then up at Sir Bors.

"It will be a wonderful day," she said, under her breath. "The most wonderful day that the knights of the Round Table have ever seen."

"We have had many adventures," replied Sir Bors. "We have seen the Fairy Hunt and followed the great white stag! We have slain giants and killed terrible beasts. We have wandered in the Enchanted Forest and seen the fairy salmon and ridden on his back. What is this adventure that will come with Galahad – who is to grow up into such a wonderful knight?"

But still neither the King nor the Princess would answer. They only smiled and shook their heads, and told him to follow them up the stairs of the castle, and they would show him a sight even more wonderful than all the rest.

So up the stairs of the castle went Sir Bors, with the King and the Princess – who still carried the baby – leading the way. And, as they went, the whisperings and the rustlings began again all around them. The little birds flew with them. The staircase windows dropped purple and silver lights upon their heads. On the Princess's shoulder alighted the small white dove, and stooped, murmuring and cooing, towards the baby, drooping the little golden bowl on the three slim chains towards the child's fingers. And tiny Galahad woke up, and caught at the pretty shining thing, and cried out delightedly. While, just ahead of the procession, it seemed to Sir Bors that the spirit of the strange castle, or whoever that lovely lady might be, moved dimly yet brightly, with the Silver Cup held in her white fingers, and the golden light that came from the candle flame shining on her face and hands and hair.

They went on – up and up and up. Then, just under the high roof of the castle, they came to a closed door all studded with strong iron nails. The maiden vanished, and Sir Bors thought she had slipped through the door just as a moonbeam might slip through the glass of a window. But the King brought out a great gold key from his pocket and put it into the lock. He turned it with a grating sound and pushed the door wide open.

Then, though all was dark on the staircase, a great light, like the light of a summer day, poured out of the room under the castle roof. The little birds flew in as if they had found their home, and the white dove which was perched on the Princess's shoulder, spread its wings and followed the rest. They all started singing with a sound as if they had settled among the blossoming branches of trees; and the scent of flowers – Sir Bors thought it was like almond blossom – came out of the room together with their music. But, when he peeped in, expecting somehow to see a garden, he saw – what do you think?

Why, just a room full of shadows; and, in the midst of the room, a table exactly like the Round Table in every way, except that, instead of being made of oak, it was made of the brightest, purest silver. And, in the middle, stood Joseph's lost Shining Cup!

Sir Bors stood and drank in the beautiful sight. Then, because he could stand it no longer – for he seemed to be in the heart of some place that was far more beautiful than Fairlyand – he hid his face in his hands. When he uncovered his eyes again, King Pelles had closed the door and Princess Elaine was singing the baby to sleep on the stairs.

"Go back to King Arthur," said the King. "Tell him what you have seen, and bid all the knights of the Round Table to wait for the coming of Galahad."

CHAPTER TWENTY

KING ARTHUR IN THE CASTLE PERILOUS

fter King Arthur, and King Pellinore, and Sir Gawaine had followed the mysterious hunt into the Enchanted Forest, they never knew at what hour of the day – or of the night, either – they might hear the horns of Fairyland blowing and catch a glimpse of the long string of black hounds streaming through the meadow grass after the beautiful white stag. Many and wonderful were the adventures that befell them – and not only them, but all the other knights of the Round Table. Sometimes, the Fairy Hunt led them into startling danger, sometimes into strange and beautiful places; but always they found that there was a lady in distress to be rescued, a giant to be killed, a brave gentleman to be helped, or something else to be done that was included in the Vow.

Well, one day, Arthur was hunting with his knights on the borders of the Enchanted Forest, following a big stag, which was not, however, the one with the fairy hoofs that shone so brightly upon the moss. The King rode his horse far from his companions, and presently overtook the fine stag, and shot it with a strong arrow from his bow. The stag fell by the side of a river, and Arthur dismounted to see if it were quite dead. As he stood there, the dim thrilling notes of the elfin horns came to him, and all at once, on the opposite side of the water, he caught a glimpse of the flying white deer of Fairyland and of the shadowy speeding bodies of the coal-black hounds.

Arthur's horse began to tremble. In another moment, it had broken free and was galloping home as fast as it could. It might well be frightened, for, as the Fairy Hunt disappeared into the shadows of the forest, the whole woods, went suddenly quite dark, while, down the glimmering black waters of the river, a little ship came sailing, with a hundred torches burning in a hundred silver holders, lighting it from end to end. Nobody was steering or guiding the ship, but it sailed on as if a clever hand were at the helm. When it reached the place where Arthur stood, it swung around on the water and lay rocking, as if it were at anchor, close against the bank where the willows grew.

"Now here is my adventure!" said King Arthur to himself, quite joyful and fearless.

In his green hunting-dress, he strode down through the willows and boarded the ship. Off it floated again, the moment he was aboard. And, when he looked up at the sails above his head, he saw that they were all made of white silk, embroidered with pink roses and blood-red poppies.

The little ship went on down the river, and the flaming torches were mirrored in the dark stream like so many stars. The King seemed to be quite alone on board, when, all at once, rising up, as it seemed, from the water, twelve beautiful maidens appeared. They made a ring around him, joining hands, and dancing as prettily as fairies do dance on a moonlit night. Then they all fell on their knees and said how glad they were that he had boarded the little ship, and what a beautiful feast was spread for him, if he would go below. So below King Arthur went, and found a cabin hung with white satin, and silver candlesticks with clear-burning candles set on a table spread with fruit and honey, white bread and red wine. He sat down to eat, and the twelve beautiful maidens waited on him. When he had finished, they led him to a bedroom hung with crimson satin, and he lay down on a blue and silver bed and fell asleep.

But, when he awoke, the pretty ship and the bed had all disappeared! He found himself in a dark dungeon, lying on a stone floor, with twenty other knights, who were all groaning in the deepest trouble and asking each other if nobody would ever come to help them.

King Arthur sat up and rubbed his eyes. "Where am I?" he asked the knights. "And who are all of you?"

*Chapter Sixteen: The Knight of the
Sparrow-Hawk*

The ragged old man invited the knight into
the ruined palace, where he was met by an
old woman, also in rags, but sweet and
dignified. With her was their daughter,
whose face and hair were very beautiful
above her poor, rough clothing.

*Chapter Sixteen: The Knight of the
Sparrow-Hawk*

A maiden, beautiful in spite of her rags,
walked quietly beside Sir Geraint as he
entered the field on his old, half-lame
horse, ready to do battle with the Knight of
the Sparrow-Hawk.

"Alas! Alas!" cried all the twenty at once. "We are prisoners, and we have been thrown into this dungeon by the cruel lord of the castle. And here he will keep us until we die. For we can only be rescued when a knight has been found who is brave enough and strong enough to fight with the lord of the castle and to conquer him. And that nobody is ever likely to do."

"But, indeed, there is now a knight among you who is quite brave enough and strong enough to try!" cried King Arthur. "Tell me how to get out of this dungeon, and I will soon challenge the lord of the castle to fight!"

Even as he said the words, a light seemed to appear from nowhere, and he saw a beautiful girl dressed like a Princess, standing beside him.

"Follow me!" said the maiden. "I am the Princess of this castle. And I want these poor prisoners saved."

Immediately, King Arthur sprang to his feet and followed her.

She led him out of the dungeon, and all the knights rose to their feet and followed. She took them to the hall of the castle and gave King Arthur armour to wear over his green hunting clothes. And she pointed to a war-horse that stood in the courtyard outside.

"Mount the horse!" said she. "Take your sword, your shield, and your spear! The lord of the castle is in the meadow on his great black steed, waiting for someone to do battle with him for his prisoners!"

Arthur was already armed, and he had taken up his shield and spear. But when he looked at the sword, he shook his head.

"I cannot fight with that sword!" he cried. "Alas! Where is my magic sword, Excalibur?"

Then the beautiful lady laughed, put her hand behind her, and brought out what looked like Arthur's own sword, Excalibur! And the King, with great joy, took it into his hand and set off for the meadow, with all the twenty knights.

This was, indeed, a great adventure – much greater than King Arthur knew. For the ship was a witch's ship, and the twelve dancing fairies were wicked fairies, and the lady who called herself the Princess of the Castle Perilous was the wickedest fairy of them all. Because, you must know, Morgan-la-Fée, Arthur's sister, had made herself Queen of the Water-Witches, and she wished her brother, the King, to be killed. So she had set all this magic afoot and had also stolen Arthur's real sword, Excalibur, and given it to the knight who was waiting for the King in the meadow.

When he saw Arthur coming, he rode towards him with a great shout, waving the stolen Excalibur round and round his head. The King spurred his own horse forward, and the two met with a ringing crash of steel. Over and over again, they struck at each other, but King Arthur felt, with anguish, his own sword was not striking keen and true. Then, even in the thick of the battle, he found time to gaze at the jewels in the scabbard of the sword his enemy used. And, all at once, the King guessed that some treachery was at work – that the other knight was fighting with Excalibur, and that the sword in his own hands was not made of fighting steel.

As Arthur realized this, he wavered in his saddle and almost fell. The wicked lord who fought him swung Excalibur high to strike the last blow. But, at that very moment, the waters of the river which flowed around the meadow were strangely disturbed. Out of the sparkling foam sprang a figure no less sparkling, and across the grass swept a beautiful lady, with dripping golden hair, and a long trailing silver gown. It was the water-fairy who had brought up Sir Lancelot, and who had heard from the moor-hens and little fishes of the plot made by Morgan-la-Fée, and was hurrying to the rescue.

She swept past the twenty knights and stood poised on her little white feet just above the grass, half-resting on the meadow flowers and half-hanging, on her misty wings, in the air. She waved her white hands and cried out magical words. And the wicked lord on the big horse dropped Excalibur into Arthur's very hands! The King seized his own good sword, and, with a shout of victory, stabbed his enemy through the breast. The big knight fell to the ground and lay there.

His servants came running from the castle and took him in. He got better in the end, but nobody cared much about that. What everybody did care about was that the twenty imprisoned knights were set free and went joyfully home to their twenty faithful wives!

CHAPTER TWENTY ONE

SIR LANCELOT OF THE LAKE

A few chapters back, you read about the baby Prince who was stolen by the water-fairy. He was very happy in the enchanted city at the bottom of the lake, the pet of all the water-fairies, but the very particular pet of the Queen. In time, he grew into a tall, handsome youth. The Queen knew that she could not keep him with her forever, and so she put him in the care of a woodman who lived in the forest that grew all around the waters of the enchanted lake. Every morning, the Lady of the Lake would take him up, up, up through the green waters, and set him upon the flowery bank, and call the woodman to come from his home and lead the boy into the forest to spend the day. But, because the lake was a part of Fairyland, Lancelot never knew that the fine city where he lived was really beneath the water. He imagined that he just walked out of it into the forest through the mists of the morning and returned to it at night through the moonlight and falling dew. But the lady whom he loved like his own mother always stood on the edge of the morning mist to wave him forward, and waited under the moonbeams, of an evening, to welcome him home.

In the forest, the woodman taught him all the craft of a huntsman. Lancelot grew clever and strong. He could shoot an arrow straight and true, shoe and saddle a horse, and climb the crags as high as the eagle's nest. How wonderful life seemed to him, lived as the forest people lived it! How firm his muscle grew, how bright his eyes, how vigorous his frame!

Then, one day, as he hunted with the forest people, he heard them talking of a great King who was named Arthur, and who was the head of a gallant company of gentlemen who called themselves the knights of the Round Table. Wonderful stories were told of these knights – of their courage, their beauty, and their pride. All that night, Lancelot lay awake, thinking about Arthur; and the next morning, as the sweet water fairy led him to the misty horizon that lay beyond the enchanted city, he told her of what he had heard, and said that nothing, nothing, could ever make him happy unless he could go to Arthur's court and become a knight of the Round Table.

"Son of a King," said the water-fairy, half sadly, half triumphantly, "I have guessed that this would be your destiny! I have known I could not keep you always. But can you be brave enough to join Arthur's knighthood! Can you, forever, be courteous, without baseness, kind to all, pitiful to the sad, generous to the poor, stern to the guilty – and choose death, at any time, before disgrace?"

Lancelot cried out that, indeed, he could. So then this Lady of the Lake bent her head and consented. And, from that moment, the preparations of Lancelot's departure began.

And such preparations they were! The water-fairy had a suit of armour made for him, all of silver and pearls. She gave him a sword, long and shining, and a white satin mantle, trimmed with ermine. Then she dressed herself, also, in a robe of gleaming white satin, with ermine and silver upon the sleeves and hem. She chose her prettiest maidens and her sprightliest pages; and she brought her fairy horses out of their fairy stalls. From the enchanted palace, she took long rolls of silk; she had the silk made into tents, for shelter on the way. Then, with songs and music, the beautiful procession set off, passed through the mists that lay on the borders of their Fairyland, and rode through the forests and meadows of West-over-the-Sea on their way to the castle of Camelot.

Arthur was coming back from hunting when he saw this sparkling company, which moved towards him through the twilight. Astonished, he drew in his horse and waited. Then, though he did not recognize her, the Lady of the Lake rode forward, in advance of the rest, as softly as a pale moth might flit across the dusky grass. Behind the fairy rode young Lancelot, all silvery-white in his armour and royal mantle.

The fairy paused as she reached Arthur's side and looked very earnestly at the astonished King. Then she waved to Lancelot to draw near also.

"Son of a King!" she said to Arthur. "I have brought you a good knight and true. He, also, is the son of a King. Admit him to your fellowship, I pray you, and make him a knight of the Round Table."

Arthur turned in his saddle, and fixed his eyes gravely upon the youth in the shining armour.

"He is only a boy," said the King. "Is he ready to prove himself? Has he done battle, yet, in any just cause? Has he suffered for the sake of the weak, protected the innocent, or punished the guilty?"

"Not yet," answered the fairy gently. "But it is his most earnest wish to do so."

Arthur turned to Sir Gawaine, who sat on his horse by the King's side.

"Take the boy to your chamber," said Arthur. "Let him watch by his armour tonight, in the chapel by the castle. Then, tomorrow, bring him to me."

He saluted the fairy, still not recognizing this beautiful and gracious lady who had brought her son to be a knight of the Round Table. He had no idea, at the moment, that she was a fairy at all, the one who had saved him and was cousin to the very fairy who had stretched a white hand and arm out of the water to give him his sword, Excalibur. The lady bent from her white horse, kissed Lancelot, and placed a ring from her own hand upon his finger.

"Take this ring," said she. "Wear it always in battle. If you are hard-pressed by an enemy, turn it upon your finger. It will make you invisible. Turn it again, and your armour will change from silver to black, from black to green, from green again to silver. Goodbye, dear son of a King! Goodbye!"

She kissed him again and rode back to the white and starry company who waited for her in the gathering night. Then they all rode silently away, and the sparkle of them died out among the trees. But Lancelot, in his silver regalia, followed the King, and Sir Gawaine, and the others into the castle of Camelot.

Sir Gawaine took him to his chamber, gave him meat and wine, and set him to watch his arms in the chapel, which all those who desired knighthood had to do. The next day, he took him to Arthur.

And now the tournament of the day was announced, and the King said that Lancelot might take his part in it. So the young Prince from the enchanted lake mounted his horse and rode with the other knights into the meadow, where very soon a great mock battle began.

How they wrestled, and fought, and clashed swords, and galloped their horses! It was one of the finest tournaments ever seen, and, very soon, all who were watching began to speak of the wonderful courage and cleverness of a young strange knight in silver that shone like sea-foam and stars. But, even while they were speaking, he disappeared, and a black knight was seen in his place, looking like some strange figure carved in ebony. Then the black knight vanished in his turn, and a knight in green appeared, like some magician of the forest. In another moment, this knight of the woodlands was gone, and there was the silver knight again, flashing across the meadow like a beautiful comet! And so on, and so on! For the black knight, and the silver knight, and the knight in emerald green were, all and each of them, none other than Lancelot of the Lake, who was continually turning his magic ring!

At last, the mock battle was over, and there was a great call for the silver knight, and the black knight, and the knight in emerald green. But only the silver knight came forward – and in his hand he held the trophies of all three!

The people who had watched the tournament knew that some fairy had been helping the silver knight in some mysterious way. So they were full of respect for him and cried out that he must indeed be made a knight of the Round Table, drink the cup of fellowship, and join in the great Vow. And the Queen smiled, as she looked on, while the King knighted him, and, in memory of the water-fairy, named him Sir Lancelot of the Lake.

CHAPTER TWENTY TWO
SIR PERCEVAL'S ADVENTURE

ir Perceval was the seventh son of King Pellinore, and, because he was the youngest, his mother loved him best. She was very glad that he was too young to go to the wars with his father and brothers. She wanted him to stay in the meadows near the castle always, playing among the flowers. But little Perceval was active and vigorous. He taught himself skill and strength by running in the forest, by breaking sticks from the strong trees, and by throwing them cleverly at targets which he invented. And one day, he saw three of the shining knights of the Round Table riding through the woods.

He watched them pass in breathless excitement, and then ran to his mother, and, describing these bright strangers, asked her who they could be. Now, the Queen knew that they were knights, but she told him they must be angels, hoping he would forget about them. But young Perceval squared his shoulders. "If those are angels, then I will be an angel, too," said he. And he set off after the knights.

He found them resting in a green glade, with their

horses tethered to the trees; and they told him they were no angels, but knights from Arthur's court. Then the boy examined their arms and watched them wistfully when they saddled their steeds again and rode away. He was determined to join them, so he took a strange old piebald horse from a field nearby, pressed a pack into the form of a saddle, and twisted some supple twigs into the shape of a bit and bridle. Then, looking the funniest rider you ever saw, he trotted off to his mother, told her that the shining visitors were not angels, but knights, and that, as he was now nearly very grown up, he meant to join them.

His mother wept bitterly, but, when she saw he was determined, she said that no King's son could go to Arthur's court in that get-up. She gave him a suit of armour, and a good horse, with as royal a saddle and bridle as he could wish. Then she kissed him goodbye and watched him set off – quite alone.

He rode for several days, through the deep forests and over high granite hills. And presently, he saw the towers of Camelot in a valley.

Now, wonderful things were happening in Arthur's kingdom just then. Strange fires were seen, at night, burning on the tops of the mountains, and sometimes flickering deep in the forest glades. Voices, and the music of harps, were heard when the moon was full. In the evenings, when Arthur's knights gathered about the Round Table, a radiance would sometimes fall upon the Seat Perilous, and the fiery letters that spelt its name would show again, as they had shown in Merlin's time. And sometimes, other writing glimmered there as well – writing which said that the time was coming when the Seat Perilous would be filled. All these things made the people of the court wonder and talk in whispers together, asking what signs so strange could mean.

Well, among the ladies of the court was a beautiful maiden, who had been born quite mute. Her lips were red, and sweet, and soft, but they had never formed a single word. She sat all day over her embroidery with quiet eyes and drooping head. But she always seemed to be listening – listening for somebody who did not come.

She was seated by the castle window when young Perceval rode through the gate. As her quick ears heard his horse's hoofs, she raised her head swiftly. A great flush of joy swept her pale face, and she laid her embroidery down. Then she stood up and, going into the hall, hid herself behind a curtain near the door.

Perceval was met in the courtyard by a knight, who, when he heard the young rider's name, led him straight to Arthur and told the King that Pellinore's son had come to ask for knighthood. Arthur summoned Perceval, but almost laughed to see him so young. He knighted him, however, for his father's sake. But, when the time came for the feast to be held at the Round Table that evening, the King bade Perceval go and sit with the young unproved knights at the end of the hall. "For," said he, "you are not yet old enough, nor strong enough, to sit at the Round Table and to join in the great Vow."

Then Perceval was very downcast. He walked slowly down the great hall, and seated himself among the lesser knights. But, all at once, he heard a murmur run through the banqueting room. Out from behind the tapestry came the beautiful mute girl, and, as she walked towards him, she spoke aloud.

"Rise up from your seat, Sir Perceval, the noble and chosen knight, and come with me!"

She took him by the hand, and he rose and walked with her up the long hall, while everybody watched in amazed silence. She led him to the seat at the right of the Seat Perilous, and pointed with her slender finger.

"Fair knight, take here your seat!" said she. "For that seat belongs to you and to none other."

Then she went away as quickly as she had come and disappeared from the palace forever. As for Sir Perceval, he stood by the seat, shy and hesitating. But King Arthur himself rose, and, going to the young knight, took him by the hand.

"Do not be afraid, Sir Perceval," he said. "We, the King and the knights of the Round Table, have

Chapter Seventeen: The Little Prince of the Lake

The beautiful fairy had taken the baby prince to a large jagged rock that jutted out from the land toward the middle of the lake.

Chapter Seventeen: The Little Prince of the Lake

The tiny baby prince woke up in the
enchanted city under the water and smiled
at the pretty water-fairies all around him.

watched the mute maiden sitting day by day, and hour by hour. We knew that she waited for somebody. And now, as everyone has heard, her lips have opened at last. Who is there who shall not listen and believe when the mute speak? Take your place next to the Seat Perilous!"

Then Sir Perceval sat down next to the Seat Perilous, and, as he did so, the far-off fires on the hills appeared again, and leapt into higher flames, and seemed to reach up to the very stars. The singing that people heard in the sky swept down to the roofs of Camelot and around the windows of the banqueting hall. The voices of the knights, as they stood shoulder to shoulder and hand to hand, rang out in the words of the great Vow and came to a sudden stop. It seemed to them as if something ought to be added to the Vow today, but what it was they did not yet understand.

The time was coming, however, when everything was to be made plain.

CHAPTER TWENTY THREE
THE COMING OF GALAHAD

ll the knights of the Round Table were at supper one evening when the adventure of Sir Galahad began. It began with a lady on a white horse, who rode in at the open doorway, calling for Sir Lancelot of the Lake. King Arthur pointed him out, and she beckoned to him with a queenly hand and told him to follow her. So away they rode into the forest, the lady in front.

She reminded him of his own fairy of long ago, as she moved on, pale and beautiful, among the shadowy trees. Presently, they came to a great building, and the lady dismounted and gave her horse to a page who hastened out to meet them. Sir Lancelot dismounted, too; and the lady waved goodbye (he was almost sure, now, it was his own fairy) and disappeared into the building. Then, after a few moments, came a sound of singing, and a procession of women, in white hoods, swept out through the gates. In the middle of the procession walked a youth, slim, upright, and very fair.

"And who may you be?" asked Sir Lancelot, taking his hand.

The good women made answer for him. They all spoke together, and their voices rustled through the trees like a soft wind.

"His name is Galahad!" they said. "His mother, the Princess Elaine, put him in our care long ago. We have brought him up among everything that is fair and innocent. He is as beautiful as the young thorn-tree that grew from Joseph's staff, and as pure as the snow that lies on its branches on Christmas Day. Take him to Arthur's court, and ask Sir Bors if he remembers the baby in the Castle of the Hidden Grail!"

Then Sir Lancelot looked at Galahad, and the boy met his glance with quiet, frank eyes. The good women said goodbye to him, and, sighing a little, went back into the castle, two and two together. And, all through the night, Sir Lancelot and Galahad rested under the forest trees. At dawn, Sir Lancelot drew his sword and made the youth a knight, under the shining of the morning star, saying:

"May you be good forever, Sir Galahad, for you are the most beautiful knight I have ever seen."

Sir Galahad lifted his face to the dawn and smiled. But when Sir Lancelot would have taken him straight to Camelot, he shook his head.

"Not yet," he said. "I will come at Whitsuntide."

So he went away through the brightening morning, and Sir Lancelot watched until he was out of sight.

Then the older knight rode back to Arthur's court, reaching Camelot just as the evening shadows were falling, and the knights were gathering together as usual around the Round Table.

Then, before they all sat down, the same thing happened that had happened at the King's wedding banquet many, many years ago. Every seat began to glow with letters of shining gold, which spelled out the name of the knight who always sat there. And upon the Seat Perilous, the letters flamed brightest and purest of all. But they read differently from the old mysterious warning, and the knights and barons reading, spoke to each other in grave whispers.

"The many, many years that Merlin told us were to pass before this seat might be filled have passed away."

King Arthur drew near and looked at the letters for a long, long time. He remembered many things that Merlin had told him before the great wizard fell asleep in Broceliande. At last, he turned to his own place at the Round Table.

"Cover the Seat Perilous with a silken covering," he commanded. "Let no one touch it nor go too near. Something is about to happen to our great company that will be beautiful and strange."

Even as he spoke, a rider galloped up to the door, and springing from his horse, clanked in among the knights, crying breathlessly: "Sirs! Sirs! A great adventure is awaiting you all." When they asked what it was, he answered that, on the waters of the river, a vast stone that looked like red marble was floating, and that in it was stuck a fair rich sword, with a handle of precious stones. And where was the knight for whom the sword was intended if not among those of the Round Table at Camelot?

Then all the knights, and the King, and the Queen, went down to the river, and, sure enough, there was the red stone floating, with the bright sword in the middle of it. Sir Lancelot, Sir Bors, Sir Geraint, Sir Gawaine, Sir Perceval, all tried to draw the sword out, but in vain. So they went back to the darkening banqueting hall, where they seemed to hear strange voices whispering near the doors and windows. These, as the company entered, closed of themselves. As they closed, a bright light, like a summer morning, filled the hall, and a smell of hawthorn blossoms drifted through it, with the song of merry birds. Then, before the knights had recovered from their wonder, they saw standing among them an old man with a long white beard, who had two strange bright snakes twisting around his neck and a harp in his hands. By his side stood Sir Galahad, dressed all in crimson satin, with a mantle of ermine hanging from his shoulders and an empty scabbard at his side.

The old man stood close to the Seat Perilous, and he raised the silken covering with his frail white hand. Then everybody saw that the golden letters had changed a third time. "This is the place of Sir Galahad, the High Prince," ran the beautiful writing. And the old man took Sir Galahad's hand and drew him to the wonderful seat.

As the young fair knight took his place, a long murmer of admiration and gladness ran around the table, and King Arthur cried out, aloud:

"It is for Sir Galahad that the sword is waiting – the sword which is fastened to the red marble stone that floats upon the stream! Old man, you have Merlin's look – Merlin's long white beard – Merlin's wonderful wise eyes! Tell us, is this not so?"

The old man bowed his head, struck his harp, and began to sing. He sang the story of Joseph, of the Rich Fisher, of the Silver Table, and of the Shining Cup. He sang of all that the Round Table meant, and of the new adventure to which the knights must vow themselves from that day – an adventure, not of lovely ladies, nor cruel giants, nor strange fairy hunts, but a search, a quest, for the treasure which had once been hidden in the strange stone castle where Sir Galahad was born. This young pure knight – so sang the old man – was the first Knight of the Grail. Now all the other knights of the Round Table must follow in his steps. Only the pure, the true, the good, could ever find the lost treasure. Sir Bors had had a glimpse of it – so, too, had Sir Perceval, Sir

Lancelot, and others. But to Sir Galahad alone had it been just part of his daily life.

All the time the old man sang, Sir Galahad sat in the Seat Perilous, his hand on his empty scabbard. Then he rose, and went out of the banqueting hall, and down to the river, which flowed black and silver through the night. The stone rocked softly on it, and the handle of the sword glowed above. Sir Galahad drew it from the red marble and went back.

Then the knights all sprang to their feet and acclaimed him, for they saw the fairy sword in his hand. As they shouted their joy in him, the hall went quite dark again, and everybody was, all at once, very quiet. For, among the shadows, a flame like the flame of a candle could be seen.

The slim flame grew and grew, until it became a great soft light. In the red heart of it moved a spirit who looked like the mute maiden. She floated through the hall, and her feet made no sound. In her hands, she held aloft the Shining Cup of the Grail.

The vision lasted only a minute before it faded. Then everything was dark again. But, in the hush, the old man began to sing once more, and the moon, suddenly shining through the window, showed Sir Galahad all in silver; the strange bright snakes that twisted about the old minstrel's neck; and the great company of shadowy knights seated at the Round Table, listening to the Song of the Holy Grail.

CHAPTER TWENTY FOUR

THE PASSING OF
THE KING

verything was different, somehow, at King Arthur's court since the coming of Sir Galahad. The knights were all vowed, now, to the search for the Holy Grail, which had disappeared from the castle of King Pelles when Sir Galahad went away. Who had taken it? Everybody asked each other, but no one could give a reply. Had it really been carried through the banqueting hall the night that Sir Galahad had taken his place upon the Seat Perilous? Or was it only a dream, a vision, that the knights had seen? If it were a vision, would any of them see it again? They could not answer these questions; but, one and all, they sought for the Shining Cup for the rest of their lives.

Joseph and the Rich Fisher had long ago passed away, you see; and perhaps they alone knew what the Holy Grail really was. The strange old minstrel with the two bright snakes around his neck knew just a litte, but not everything. He wore the snakes to show that he belonged to the old, old order of bards – the men who were something like priests and who sang stories of great nations and greater kings. His Song of the Holy Grail was written down in the little book that he must have found in Merlin's mysterious house, with the seventy windows and the sixty doors. For Merlin was one of these bards himself, and he very likely wore bright snakes about his neck as he came and went at King Arthur's court, though we are not exactly told that he ever did. But, then, we are by no means told all that happened in those days, and, if we were, perhaps we should not believe it. This we do know, however; that all the knights who searched for the lost Grail Cup knew that they had no chance of finding it, or even catching a glimpse of it in a vision, unless they were perfectly good and true and pure and without reproach. So all of them tried hard to be so; and, though none of them ever quite succeeded, the very trying made their lives beautiful – just as shining and beautiful as the silver armour they wore, and the spears and swords that they carried in their hands.

They still met at the Round Table, still passed the Cup of Fellowship from hand to hand, but the King, as he sat among them, felt that he was growing old. His eyes were often heavy, and his feet and hands were tired. And, one day, he was obliged to go into battle against an enemy when he was too weary to fight. He was struck down and wounded, and his faithful knights carried him to a quiet grassy place in a meadow, near which rippled the shining waters of a great lake.

King Arthur lay on the moss with his fingers on the handle of his sword Excalibur, and his followers stood around him with sad faces, for they thought that Death was about to take their beloved King. But he himself knew better. He smiled as he lay there, and his face was very bright. Lifting himself up a little, he looked towards the waters of the lake, and then he beckoned to a knight who was called Sir Bedivere.

"Take my sword Excalibur," said he. "Throw it as far as you can fling it towards the middle of the lake. Then come back and tell me what happens."

Sir Bedivere took the sword and carried it to the edge of the lake. Night was falling, and the moon was brightening above the quiet hills. In the moonlight, the jewels in the handle of Excalibur looked very rich and beautiful – so rich and so beautiful that Sir Bedivere felt he could not bear to throw the sword into the water. He hid it all among the forget-me-nots and meadow-sweet, and went, empty-handed, back to the King.

"Did you throw the sword into the lake?" asked Arthur eagerly.

"Yes, sire," answered Sir Bedivere boldly.

"What happened?"

"Nothing happened, sire!"

The King lay back again with a groan.

"Faithless messenger!" he said. "You have not thrown the sword! Go! Do as I command."

Again Sir Bedivere went, but again the beauty of Excalibur overcame him. He returned to the King and declared that he had flung the sword into the water, but still nothing had happened.

Arthur looked at him steadily, and his eyes made Sir Bedivere afraid.

"You are not speaking the truth!" cried the King. "Go! Do as I command!"

His voice was very strong and stern, and at last Bedivere obeyed. Hurrying to the water's edge, he took Excalibur in his hand again, without daring to look at its beauty. The rubies and sapphires and diamonds of the handle flashed as he flung it far, far into the lake. Just as it was about to strike the water, a white hand and arm, clothed in a shining sleeve, rose above the ripples, and the outstreched fingers caught the sword by he hilt. Three times, the hand waved Excalibur in the moonlight – and both arm and sword disappeared below the water, and all was still.

Breathless and awed, Sir Bedivere went back to the King and told what he had seen.

"It is well!" said Arthur. "Carry me to the lake!"

So his knights lifted him and carried him gently across the moonlit grass until they came to the water's edge. As they walked in slow procession, they saw a dim ship, like a dark barge, coming from the middle of the lake towards the bank. Many ladies, shadowy in the pale light, were seated in it, with their heads bowed upon their hands. All of them were hooded; and three, who wore crowns upon the heads, looked like Queens.

Then the King bade the knights lay him in the barge, and they did so and gave him into the care of the three Queens. Down from the hills swept a great wind – and it seemed as if the sound of sobbing and wailing was in its cold breath. The clouds rushed across the moon, and the water of the lake looked black and terrible as the barge began to move away from the land. The knights stood upon the bank and watched as if they were in a dream.

Then, even as they watched, the darkness went away. Far, far off, right away, as it were, beyond the lake, little shining islands began to appear, bright and beautiful, looking for all the world like sunset clouds. All the knights had heard of these islands and knew that they were called the Isles of the Blest. In the very heart of them was the fairest of all, named Avalon. Its valleys were fragrant with flowers, and in its orchard grew trees that bore golden apples. It seemed to the knights that the barge with the three fairy Queens and the weary human King sailed right up to the shores of Avalon, and that a number of bright and beautiful people came to meet it. Then the whole vision faded. Nothing was left but the lake, and the moonlit meadows, and the memory of the great and only King of the Round Table.

But some people say that Arthur lives and is happy in Avalon to this day, and that there he has met Joseph, and the Rich Fisher, and his old wise teacher, Merlin, the great magician. They say, too, that it is in Avalon that the Silver Table is hidden, on which stands the Shining Cup; and that the mysterious feast is held there every evening, which fills all the guests with joy and amazement, just as they were filled with joy and amazement hundreds of years ago on that Christmas Day when Joseph's staff broke into blossom at Glastonbury.

Chapter Nineteen: The Adventure of Sir Bors

In the heart of the golden light appeared a slim and beautiful lady. She seemed to be a sort of delicate spirit, and she moved like a spirit through the dim shadows of the hall.

Chapter Twenty: King Arthur in the
Castle Perilous

The King seized his own precious sword, Excalibur, and with a shout of victory, stabbed his enemy, the lord of the Castle Perilous, through the heart.

Chapter Twenty One: Sir Lancelot of the Lake

The Queen of the Water-Fairies held the young Lancelot in her arms, calling him "Son of a King". Then, every day, he left the enchanted city under the water to learn the ways of men and the world.

Chapter Twenty One: Sir Lancelot of the Lake

The handsome youth learned the craft of the huntsman well. He could shoot an arrow straight and true, shoe and saddle a horse, and climb the crags as high as an eagle's nest.

THE COMING OF ARTHUR

The legends of the handsome King Arthur and his gallant knights are among the most popular stories in English literature. They have been told and retold over the centuries by writers and poets since the Dark Ages.

The first storytellers were probably troubadors, or bards, who came from Wales or the southwest of England. An English writer, Geoffrey of Monmouth, created a written version in the twelfth century, and in the 1400s, Sir Thomas Mallory retold Geoffrey's version and incorporated other stories which had been added by early French poets. In the nineteenth century, Alfred, Lord Tennyson, the English poet laureate, wrote a series of related poems about the legendary King, his beautiful queen Guinevere, and the courtly knights who took their places at the Round Table.

On the following pages, you can read "The Coming of Arthur", from Tennyson's *Idylls of the King*, in which several of the stories in this book are mentioned.

Leodogran, the King of Cameliard,
Had one fair daughter, and none other child;
And she was fairest of all flesh on earth,
Guinevere, and in her his one delight.

   For many a petty king ere Arthur came
Ruled in this isle, and ever waging war
Each upon other, wasted all the land;
And still from time to time the heathen host
Swarm'd overseas, and harried what was left.
And so there grew great tracts of wilderness,
Wherein the beast was ever more and more,
But man was less and less, till Arthur came.
For first Aurelius lived and fought and died,
And after him King Uther fought and died,
But either fail'd to make the kingdom one.
And after these King Arthur for a space,
And thro' the puissance of his Table Round,
Drew all their petty princedoms under him,
Their king and head, and made a realm,
     and reign'd.

And thus the land of Cameliard was waste,
Thick with wet woods, and many a beast therein,
And none or few to scare or chase the beast;
So that wild dog, and wolf and boar and bear
Came night and day, and rooted in the fields,
And wallow'd in the gardens of the King.
And ever and anon the wolf would steal
The children and devour, but now and then,
Her own brood lost or dead, lent her fierce teat
To human sucklings; and the children, housed
In her foul den, there at their meat would growl
And mock their foster-mother on four feet,
Till, straighten'd, they grew up to wolf-like men,
Worse than the wolves. And King Leodogran
Groan'd for the Roman legions here again,
And Cæsar's eagle: then his brother king,
Urien, assail'd him: last a heathen horde,
Reddening the sun with smoke and earth
        with blood,
And on the spike that split the mother's heart
Spitting the child, brake on him, till, amazed,
He knew not whither he should turn for aid.

But – for he heard of Arthur newly crown'd,
Tho' not without an uproar made by those
Who cried, 'He is not Uther's son' – the King
Sent to him, saying, 'Arise, and help us thou!
For here between the man and beast we die.'

And Arthur yet had done no deed of arms,
But heard the call, and came: and Guinevere
Stood by the castle walls to watch him pass;
But since he neither wore on helm or shield
The golden symbol of his kinglihood,
But rode a simple knight among his knights,
And many of these in richer arms than he,
She saw him not, or mark'd not, if she saw,
One among many, tho' his face was bare.
But Arthur, looking downward as he past,
Felt the light of her eyes into his life
Smite on the sudden, yet rode on, and pitch'd
His tents beside the forest. Then he drave
The heathen; after, slew the beast, and fell'd

The forest, letting in the sun, and made
Broad pathways for the hunter and the knight
And so return'd.

   For while he linger'd there,
A doubt that ever smoulder'd in the hearts
Of those great Lords and Barons of his realm
Flash'd forth and into war: for most of these,
Colleaguing with a score of petty kings,
Made head against him, crying, 'Who is he
That he should rule us? who hath proven him
King Uther's son? for lo! we look at him,
And find nor face nor bearing, limbs nor voice,
Are like to those of Uther whom we knew.
This is the son of Gorloïs, not the King;
This is the son of Anton, not the King.'

   And Arthur, passing thence to battle, felt
Travail, and throes and agonies of the life,
Desiring to be join'd with Guinevere;

And thinking as he rode, 'Her father said
That there between the man and beast they die.
Shall I not lift her from this land of beasts
Up to my throne, and side by side with me?
What happiness to reign a lonely king,
Vext – O ye stars that shudder over me,
O earth that soundest hollow under me,
Vext with waste dreams? for saving I be join'd
To her that is the fairest under heaven,
I seem as nothing in the mighty world,
And cannot will my will, nor work my work
Wholly, nor make myself in mine own realm
Victor and lord. But were I join'd with her,
Then might we live together as one life,
And reigning with one will in everything
Have power on this dark land to lighten it,
And power on this dead world to make it live.'

Thereafter – as he speaks who tells the tale –
When Arthur reach'd a field-of-battle bright
With pitch'd pavilions of his foe, the world
Was all so clear about him, that he saw
The smallest rock far on the faintest hill,
And even in high day the morning star.
So when the King had set his banner broad,
At once from either side, with trumpet-blast,
And shouts, and clarions shrilling unto blood,
The long-lanced battle let their horses run.
And now the Barons and the kings prevail'd,
And now the King, as here and there that war
Went swaying; but the Powers who walk
    the world
Made lightnings and great thunders over him,
And dazed all eyes, till Arthur by main might,
And mightier of his hands with every blow,
And leading all his knighthood threw the kings
Carádos, Urien, Cradlemont of Wales,
Claudias, and Clariance of Northumberland,
The King Brandagoras of Latangor,

With Anguisant of Erin, Morganore,
And Lot of Orkney. Then, before a voice
As dreadful as the shout of one who sees
To one who sins, and deems himself alone
And all the world asleep, they swerved and brake
Flying, and Arthur call'd to stay the brands
That hack'd among the flyers, 'Ho! they yield!'
So like a painted battle the war stood
Silenced, the living quiet as the dead,
And in the heart of Arthur joy was lord.
He laugh'd upon his warrior whom he loved
And honour'd most. 'Thou dost not doubt
     me King,
So well thine arm hath wrought for me to-day.'
'Sir and my liege,' he cried, 'the fire of God
Descends upon thee in the battle-field:
I know thee for my King!' Whereat the two,
For each had warded either in the fight,
Sware on the field of death a deathless love.
And Arthur said, 'Man's word is God in man:
Let chance what will, I trust thee to the death.'

Then quickly from the foughten field he sent
Ulfius, and Brastias, and Bedivere,
His new-made knights, to King Leodogran,
Saying, 'If I in aught have served thee well,
Give me thy daughter Guinevere to wife.'

Whom when he heard, Leodogran in heart
Debating – 'How should I that am a king,
'However much he holp me at my need,
Give my one daughter saving to a king,
And a king's son? – lifted his voice, and call'd
A hoary man, his chamberlain, to whom
He trusted all things, and of him required
His counsel: 'Knowest thou aught of
      Arthur's birth?'

Then spake the hoary chamberlain and said,
'Sir King, there be but two old men that know:
And each is twice as old as I; and one
Is Merlin, the wise man that ever served
King Uther thro' his magic art; and one

Is Merlin's master (so they call him) Bleys,
Who taught him magic; but the scholar ran
Before the master, and so far, that Bleys
Laid magic by, and sat him down, and wrote
All things and whatsoever Merlin did
In one great annal-book, where after-years
Will learn the secret of our Arthur's birth.'

To whom the King Leodogran replied,
'O friend, had I been holpen half as well
By this King Arthur as by thee to-day,
Then beast and man had had their share of me:
But summon here before us yet once more
Ulfius, and Brastias, and Bedivere.'

Then, when they came before him,
    the King said,
'I have seen the cuckoo chased by lesser fowl,
And reason in the chase: but wherefore now
Do these your lords stir up the heat of war,
Some calling Arthur born of Gorloïs,
Others of Anton? Tell me, ye yourselves,
Hold ye this Arthur for King Uther's son?'

And Ulfius and Brastias answer'd, 'Ay.'
Then Bedivere, the first of all his knights
Knighted by Arthur at his crowning, spake –
For bold in heart and act and word was he,
Whenever slander breathed against the King –

'Sir, there be many rumours on this head:
For there be those who hate him in their hearts,
Call him baseborn, and since his ways are sweet,
And theirs are bestial, hold him less than man:
And there be those who deem him more than man,
And dream he dropt from heaven: but my belief
In all this matter – so ye care to learn –
Sir, for ye know that in King Uther's time
The prince and warrior Gorloïs, he that held
Tintagil castle by the Cornish sea,
Was wedded with a winsome wife, Ygerne:
And daughters had she borne him, – one whereof,
Lot's wife, the Queen of Orkney, Bellicent,
Hath ever like a loyal sister cleaved

To Arthur, – but a son she had not borne.
And Uther cast upon her eyes of love:
But she, a stainless wife to Gorloïs,
So loathed the bright dishonour of his love,
That Gorloïs and King Uther went to war:
And overthrown was Gorloïs and slain.
Then Uther in his wrath and heat besieged
Ygerne within Tintagil, where her men,
Seeing the mighty swarm about their walls,
Left her and fled, and Uther enter'd in,
And there was none to call to but himself.
So, compass'd by the power of the King,
Enforced she was to wed him in her tears,
And with a shameful swiftness: afterward,
Not many moons, King Uther died himself,
Moaning and wailing for an heir to rule
After him, lest the realm should go to wrack.
And that same night, the night of the new year,
By reason of the bitterness and grief
That vext his mother, all before his time

Was Arthur born, and all as soon as born
Deliver'd at a secret postern-gate
To Merlin, to be holden far apart
Until his hour should come; because the lords
Of that fierce day were as the lords of this,
Wild beasts, and surely would have torn the child
Piecemeal among them, had they known; for each
But sought to rule for his own self and hand,
And many hated Uther for the sake
Of Gorloïs. Wherefore Merlin took the child,
And gave him to Sir Anton, an old knight
And ancient friend of Uther; and his wife
Nursed the young prince, and rear'd him with
      her own;
And no man knew. And ever since the lords
Have foughten like wild beasts among themselves,
So that the realm has gone to wrack: but now,
This year, when Merlin (for his hour had come)
Brought Arthur forth, and set him in the hall,
Proclaiming, 'Here is Uther's heir, your king,'
A hundred voices cried, 'Away with him!

No king of ours! a son of Gorloïs he,
Or else the child of Anton, and no king,
Or else baseborn.' Yet Merlin thro' his craft,
And while the people clamour'd for a king,
Had Arthur crown'd; but after, the great lords
Banded, and so brake out in open war.'

Then while the King debated with himself
If Arthur were the child of shamefulness,
Or born the son of Gorloïs, after death,
Or Uther's son, and born before his time,
Or whether there were truth in anything
Said by these three, there came to Cameliard,
With Gawain and young Modred, her two sons,
Lot's wife, the Queen of Orkney, Bellicent;
Whom as he could, not as he would, the King
Made feast for, saying, as they sat at meat,

'A doubtful throne is ice on summer seas.
Ye come from Arthur's court. Victor his men

Chapter Twenty One: Sir Lancelot of the Lake

Sir Lancelot's first tournament, which he
fought dressed all in silver and wearing the
fairy-queen's magic ring, made him famous
throughout the land.

Chapter Twenty Three: The Coming of Galahad

As the knights waited breathlessly, an old
man with a long white beard appeared.
Two strange bright snakes twisted around
his neck, and he carried a harp in his
hands. By his side stood Sir Galahad,
dressed in crimson satin, with a mantle of
white ermine hanging from his shoulders
and an empty scabbard swinging
at his side.

Report him! Yea, but ye – think ye this king –
So many those that hate him, and so strong,
So few his knights, however brave they be –
Hath body enow to hold his foemen down?'

    'O King,' she cried, 'and I will tell thee: few,
Few, but all brave, all of one mind with him;
For I was near him when the savage yells
Of Uther's peerage died, and Arthur sat
Crown'd on the daïs, and his warriors cried,
"Be thou the king, and we will work thy will
Who love thee." Then the King in low deep tones,
And simple words of great authority,
Bound them by so strait vows to his own self,
That when they rose, knighted from kneeling,
        some
Were pale as at the passing of a ghost,
Some flush'd, and others dazed, as one who wakes
Half-blinded at the coming of a light.

'But when he spake and cheer's his
   Table Round
With large, divine, and comfortable words,
Beyond my tongue to tell thee – I beheld
From eye to eye thro' all their Order flash
A momentary likeness of the King:
And ere it left their faces, thro' the cross
And those around it and the Crucified,
Down from the casement over Arthur, smote
Flame-colour, vert and azure, in three rays,
One falling upon each of three fair queens,
Who stood in silence near his throne, the friends
Of Arthur, gazing on him, tall, with bright
Sweet faces, who will help him at his need.

'And there I saw mage Merlin, whose vast wit
And hundred winters are but as the hands
Of loyal vassals toiling for their liege.

'And near him stood the Lady of the Lake,
Who knows a subtler magic than his own –
Clothed in white samite, mystic, wonderful.
She gave the King his huge cross-hilted sword,
Whereby to drive the heathen out: a mist
Of incense curl'd about her, and her face
Wellnigh was hidden in the minster gloom;
But there was heard among the holy hymns
A voice as of the waters, for she dwells
Down in a deep; calm, whatsoever storms
May shake the world, and when the surface rolls,
Hath power to walk the waters like our Lord.

'There likewise I beheld Excalibur
Before him at his crowning borne, the sword
That rose from out the bosom of the lake,
And Arthur row'd across and took it – rich
With jewels, elfin Urim, on the hilt,
Bewildering heart and eye – the blade so bright
That men are blinded by it – on one side,

Graven in the oldest tongue of all this world,
"Take me," but turn the blade and ye shall see,
And written in the speech ye speak yourself,
"Cast me away!" And sad was Arthur's face
Taking it, but old Merlin counsell'd him,
"Take thou and strike! the time to cast away
Is yet far-off." So this great brand the king
Took, and by this will beat his foemen down.'

Thereat Leodogran rejoiced, but thought
To sift his doubtings to the last, and ask'd,
Fixing full eyes of question on her face,
'The swallow and the swift are near akin,
But thou art closer to this noble prince,
Being his own dear sister;' and she said,
'Daughter of Gorloïs and Ygerne am I;'
'And therefore Arthur's sister?' ask'd the King.
She answer'd, 'These be secret things,'
    and sign'd
To those two sons to pass, and let them be.
And Gawain went, and breaking into song

Sprang out, and follow'd by his flying hair
Ran like a colt, and leapt at all he saw:
But Modred laid his ear beside the doors,
And there half-heard; the same that afterward
Struck for the throne, and striking found
   his doom.

And the Queen made answer, 'What know I?
For dark my mother was in eyes and hair,
And dark in hair and eyes am I; and dark
Was Gorloïs, yea and dark was Uther too,
Wellnigh to blackness; but this King is fair
Beyond the race of Britons and of men.
Moreover, always in my mind I hear
A cry from out the dawning of my life,
A mother weeping, and I hear her say,
"O that ye had some brother, pretty one,
To guard thee on the rough ways of the world."'

'Ay,' said the King, 'and hear ye such a cry?
But when did Arthur chance upon thee first?'

'O King!' she cried, 'and I will tell thee true:
He found me first when yet a little maid:
Beaten I had been for a little fault
Whereof I was not guilty; and out I ran
And flung myself down on a bank of heath,
And hated this fair world and all therein,
And wept, and wish'd that I were dead; and he –
I know not whether of himself he came,
Or brought by Merlin, who, they say, can walk
Unseen at pleasure – he was at my side,
And spake sweet words, and comforted my heart,
And dried my tears, being a child with me.
And many a time he came, and evermore
As I grew greater grew with me; and sad
At times he seem'd, and sad with him was I,
Stern too at times, and then I loved him not,
But sweet again, and then I loved him well.
And now of late I see him less and less,
But those first days had golden hours for me,
For then I surely thought he would be king.

'But let me tell thee now another tale:
For Bleys, our Merlin's master, as they say,
Died but of late, and sent his cry to me,
To hear him speak before he left his life.
Shrunk like a fairy changeling lay the mage;
And when I enter'd told me that himself
And Merlin ever served about the King,
Uther, before he died; and on the night
When Uther in Tintagil past away
Moaning and wailing for an heir, the two
Left the still King, and passing forth to breathe,
Then from the castle gateway by the chasm
Descending thro' the dismal night – a night
In which the bounds of heaven and earth
    were lost –
Beheld, so high upon the dreary deeps
It seem'd in heaven, a ship, the shape thereof
A dragon wing'd, and all from stem to stern
Bright with a shining people on the decks,
And gone as soon as seen. And then the two
Dropt to the cove, and watch'd the great sea fall,

Wave after wave, each mightier than the last,
Till last, a ninth one, gathering half the deep
And full of voices, slowly rose and plunged
Roaring, and all the wave was in a flame:
And down the wave and in the flame was borne
A naked babe, who rode to Merlin's feet,
Who stoopt and caught the babe, and cried
   "The King!
Here is an heir for Uther!" And the fringe
Of that great breaker, sweeping up the strand,
Lash'd at the wizard as he spake the word,
And all at once all round him rose in fire,
So that the child and he were clothed in fire.
And presently thereafter follow'd calm,
Free sky and stars: "And this same child,"
   he said,
"Is he who reigns; nor could I part in peace
Till this were told." And saying this the seer
Went thro' the strait and dreadful pass of death,
Not ever to be question'd any more
Save on the further side; but when I met
Merlin, and ask'd him if these things were truth –

The shining dragon and the naked child
Descending in the glory of the seas –
He laugh'd as is his wont, and answer'd me
In riddling triplets of old time, and said:

  ' "Rain, rain, and sun! a rainbow in the sky!
A young man will be wiser by and by;
An old man's wit may wander ere he die.
  Rain, rain, and sun! a rainbow on the lea!
And truth is this to me, and that to thee;
And truth or clothed or naked let it be.
  Rain, sun, and rain! and the free
    blossom blows:
Sun, rain, and sun! and where is he who knows?
From the great deep to the great deep he goes."

  'So Merlin riddling anger'd me; but thou
Fear not to give this King thine only child,
Guinevere: so great bards of him will sing
Hereafter; and dark sayings from of old
Ranging and ringing thro' the minds of men,

THE COMING OF ARTHUR

And echo'd by old folk beside their fires
For comfort after their wage-work is done,
Speak of the King; and Merlin in our time
Hath spoken also, not in jest, and sworn
Tho' men may wound him that he will not die,
But pass, again to come; and then or now
Utterly smite the heathen underfoot,
Till these and all men hail him for their king.'

  She spake and King Leodogran rejoiced,
But musing 'Shall I answer yea or nay?'
Doubted, and drowsed, nodded and slept,
   and saw,
Dreaming, a slope of land that ever grew,
Field after field, up to a height, the peak
Haze-hidden, and thereon a phantom king,
Now looming, and now lost; and on the slope
The sword rose, the hind fell, the herd was driven,
Fire glimpsed; and all the land from roof and rick,
In drifts of smoke before a rolling wind,
Stream'd to the peak and mingled with the haze

And made it thicker; while the phantom king
Sent out at times a voice; and here or there
Stood one who pointed toward the voice, the rest
Slew on and burnt, crying, 'No king of ours,
No son of Uther, and no king of ours;'
Till with a wink his dream was changed, the haze
Descended, and the solid earth became
As nothing, but the King stood out in heaven,
Crown'd. And Leodogran awoke, and sent
Ulfius, and Brastias and Bedivere,
Back to the court of Arthur answering yea.

Then Arthur charged his warrior whom
   he loved
And honour'd most, Sir Lancelot, to ride forth
And bring the Queen; – and watch'd him from
   the gates:
And Lancelot past away among the flowers,
(For then was latter April) and return'd
Among the flowers, in May, with Guinevere.
To whom arrived, by Dubric the high saint,

Chief of the church in Britain, and before
The stateliest of her altar-shrines, the King
That morn was married, while in stainless white,
The fair beginners of a nobler time,
And glorying in their vows and him, his knights
Stood round him, and rejoicing in his joy.
Far shone the fields of May thro' open door,
The sacred altar blossom'd white with May,
The Sun of May descended on their King,
They gazed on all earth's beauty in their Queen,
Roll'd incense, and there past along the hymns
A voice as of the waters, while the two
Sware at the shrine of Christ a deathless love:
And Arthur said, 'Behold, thy doom is mine.
Let chance what will, I love thee to the death!'
To whom the Queen replied with drooping eyes,
'King and my lord, I love thee to the death!'
And holy Dubric spread his hands and spake,
'Reign ye, and live and love, and make the world
Other, and may thy Queen be one with thee,
And all this Order of thy Table Round
Fulfil the boundless purpose of their King!'

So Dubric said; but when they left the shrine
Great Lords from Rome before the portal stood,
In scornful stillness gazing as they past;
Then while they paced a city all on fire
With sun and cloth of gold, the trumpets blew,
And Arthur's knighthood sang before the King:–

'Blow trumpet, for the world is white with May;
Blow trumpet, the long night hath roll'd away!
Blow thro' the living world – "Let the King reign."

'Shall Rome or Heathen rule in Arthur's realm?
Flash brand and lance, fall battleaxe upon helm,
Fall battleaxe, and flash brand! Let the King reign.

'Strike for the King and live! his knights have
  heard
That God hath told the King a secret word.
Fall battleaxe, and flash brand! Let the King reign.

'Blow trumpet! he will lift us from the dust.
Blow trumpet! live the strength and die the lust!
Clang battleaxe, and clash brand! Let the King
   reign.

'Strike for the King and die! and if thou diest,
The King is King, and ever wills the highest.
Clang battleaxe, and clash brand! Let the King
   reign.

'Blow, for our Sun is mighty in his May!
Blow, for our Sun is mightier day by day!
Clang battleaxe, and clash brand! Let the King
   reign.

'The King will follow Christ, and we the King
In whom high God hath breathed a secret thing.
Fall battleaxe, and flash brand! Let the King reign.'

So sang the knighthood, moving to their hall.
There at the banquet those great Lords from Rome,
The slowly-fading mistress of the world,
Strode in, and claim'd their tribute as of yore.
But Arthur spake, 'Behold, for these have sworn
To wage my wars, and worship me their King;
The old order changeth, yielding place to new;
And we that fight for our fair father Christ,
Seeing that ye be grown too weak and old
To drive the heathen from your Roman wall,
No tribute will we pay:' so those great lords
Drew back in wrath, and Arthur strove with Rome.

And Arthur and his knighthood for a space
Were all one will, and thro' that strength the King
Drew in the petty princedoms under him,
Fought, and in twelve great battles overcame
The heathen hordes, and made a realm
      and reign'd.

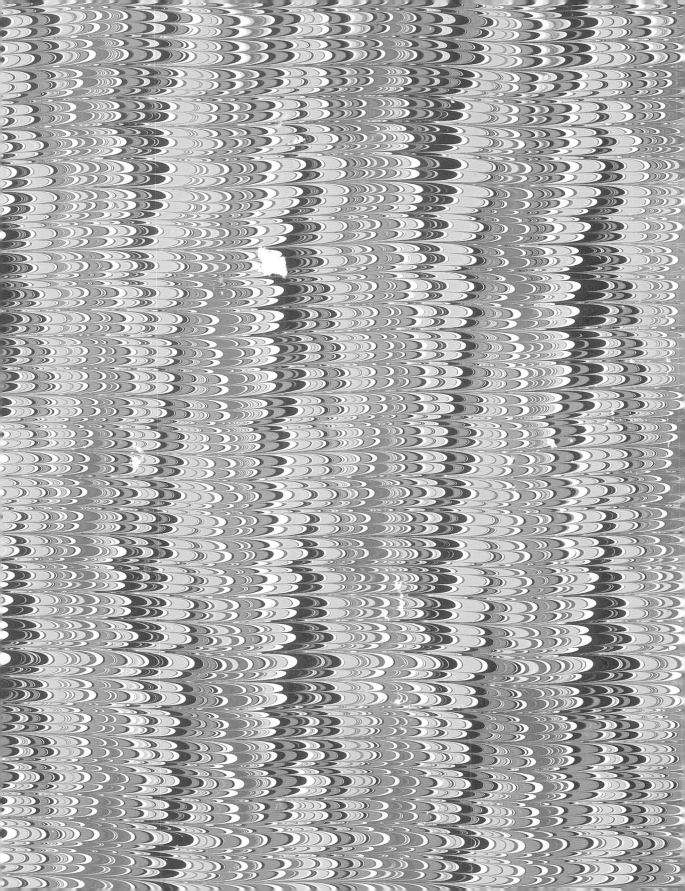